Books may be purchased in quantity and/or special sales by contacting Three Berries Publishing; 870-307-1544.

Published by: Three Berries Publishing, Batesville, Arkansas
Editing by: Adjective Solutions
Language: English
ISBN-10: 1449502857
ISBN-13: 978-1449502850
10 9 8 7 6 5 4 3 2
Second Edition

Head Lice

and

Hot Tamales

by
Luanne Gregory

Dedication

This book is dedicated to my mother, Norma Jean Baughn Boles. Life was not easy for most people who lived through the great depression, including Mom. She has the unique ability to live in the present without worrying about what might be. In almost every picture of her as a child, she had a baby in her lap or on her hip, so it's no surprise that she raised nine children, who in the words of Solomon, "rise up and call her blessed." The best gift she ever gave me was the ability to find excitement in the little things. Thanks to her, my calm life is always a wild ride!

Never Ending Thanks

Anyone who is married to a writer knows what a crazy, obsessive group of people we are. Thank goodness that my husband, Don understands my obsession and loves me in spite of them. If I ever doubt divine intervention, I just remember back to that July evening in 1980. I love you "three."

My children, Taylor, Colton and Emmie didn't know that we were different from other families until they were old enough to compare notes with their friends. We are nuts! I am so very proud of the people you have become, never blindly following the crowd but making decisions based on what you know to be right. I love you all the berries.

How could I have ever gotten this completed without my sisters, who gave up hours of their time to read, correct and critique? Ina Lee, Juda, Linda and Kat. Friends, confidants and keepers of secrets.

Disclosure

There were many times during my childhood when we could not afford a television. We didn't need one. Mother told us exciting tales of her colorful life. This book is loosely based on one of those stories. Since I was just a kid when I first heard about this summer, many of the details are now blurry. I've also added characters, deleted others, used familiar names that actually had nothing to do with this time and created parts of the tale from my very active imagination.

Prologue

"You're killing me," panic and pain infused the short muffled sentence.

"It's what you deserve," boomed the man's slurred response. "When they find your body, nobody will do a thing and nobody will care either." Leather cutting into flesh made its distinctive thwacking sound.

"Bill, the girls, the girls will hear." It was a pitiful cry, one that victims of abuse all recognize. "Please, don't do this."

"Maybe they're next. I'll sharpen my razor on the strap until it'll slit their throats without more than a whisper." His inhuman growl crept out and seeped into every crevice of the house, oozing under the bedroom door where three little girls huddled together, paralyzed with fear.

Chapter One
A Memorable Birthday

"Girls, hush up so we can hear what's happening," Momma whispered. Dessert dishes and the remains of a plain vanilla cake sat on the table in front of the sofa. Cleaning up the mess could wait a few minutes. Momma didn't want to miss a minute of the thrilling announcement.

"The killer is dead!" With the same excitement as a baseball announcer, a deep timbered voice piped the news into our home. Radio was our lifeline to the rest of the world. Our family faithfully listened to the world news each night on the big, wooden cabinet, which was the focal point of our living room. Momma, along with my two sisters and me, cheered when that radio voice announced that the law had finally gotten around to executing Richard Bruno Hauptmann for kidnapping and killing the Lindbergh baby.

Bruno. . . it sounded like a killer's name. The country had celebrated with Charles Lindbergh on his non-stop trip between New York and Paris, and we wept with his family when in '33 Bruno had kidnapped and killed Lindbergh's little boy.

"Shush, girls keep it down," Momma's voice rose over our shouts and cheers. We were always getting shushed for one thing or another.

Kidnapping was big business. For a time, it seemed that criminals had an upper hand over law enforcement. Rampaging all over the Midwest, Bonnie and Clyde Barrow were busy robbing, shooting, and kidnapping. Just like Bruno Hauptmann, they too had met with a violent end. A few years back, they were shot dead by the cops way down in Louisiana. Their deaths seemed sad to me, but Daddy said they got what they had coming. We were in a time of great hardship and some folks were tempted to take the easy road to make ends meet.

Not all the news on the radio was bad. Earlier in the year, Edward VIII had been crowned king of England, Sonja Henie won a gold medal at the Winter Olympics, and we heard the stirrings of rumors that Germany was ignoring the rules of the Treaty of Versailles. We didn't exactly know what the Treaty of Versailles was, but it all sounded important and exciting when the broadcaster with the clear, even voice announced it.

Once when the Wesley's shallow pond froze solid, we had skated on it for hours. We didn't have skates or anything, but a bunch of us kids slipped, slid and fell until we were exhausted. I sure would like to see Sonja Henie swirl around on the ice.

Word of the baby killer's execution isn't the reason that date in April sticks in my mind. Celebrating my eleventh birthday was exciting, but not nearly so much as the news we would soon receive.

I fingered the colored glass stickpin tacked to my collar. "Momma, thank you for the present," I said. The pin wasn't new. It had been in Momma's jewelry box for a long time. She had caught me admiring it too many times to count.

"You're welcome, Jean," Momma said. Just as she gave me another birthday hug, my tenth or twentieth of the day, someone started pounding on the front door.

Riley Miller didn't wait for Momma to answer; he just burst into the front room shouting, "Ms Ruby, you got to come quick. There's an important phone call."

Riley was almost a year older than me, and a constant thorn in my side. His unruly hair was plastered to his head and he was out of breath. The Millers were the only family in our neighborhood who had a telephone. They took messages for just about everybody in a five-block area. They were friends to all and landlord to many of us. Most of the neighborhood people tried not to take advantage of them. After all, they were good neighbors and our contact to the rest of the world. About six months earlier, old Mrs. Finney got a call when her daughter delivered her fifth baby, another boy. Just last week, my friend, Tennessee McCloud found out that her grandma who lived in Tennessee had died. Sometimes messages from the Millers were good news, sometimes bad.

Riley was the Millers' youngest boy, and Mrs. Miller freely admitted that she had spoiled him rotten. For just a split second, I thought that just maybe Daddy was calling to wish me happy birthday. But Riley wouldn't have worn himself out if the news had been good. My heart skipped a beat and my imagination ran wild.

For as long as I could remember, Daddy had worked for the Arkansas Highway Department. Turning dirt roads into two-lane highways was an obsession for him. Unfortunately, roadwork wasn't Daddy's only passion. He drank too much, which made him mean to Momma. Sometimes he whipped us too, but most of the time, Momma took the brunt of Daddy's rage. I almost never asked anyone to visit our home because we never knew when he might stop after work to have a drink.

The problem with Daddy's drinking was that he rarely had just one drink. Every evening, Momma watched the clock. If Daddy was more than thirty minutes late, she fed us supper and sent us to bed. Going to bed at six-thirty wasn't too bad a few times a month in the winter, but during the long summer days, it was awfully hard to get to sleep hours before the sun went down. When Daddy was on a drunk, he would tear into the house, yelling and screaming. There was nothing Momma could do to stop it. He always found something she had done wrong. My two sisters and I lay huddled in our bed while he shouted loud enough for the whole neighborhood to hear. More times than not, Momma would have a bruise or two the next day. She never said anything about what went on and neither did we. In those days, a woman with three kids didn't leave her husband just because he knocked her around some. At least, most women didn't.

The year was 1936 and while the whole country was in trouble, eastern Arkansas was in worse shape than many other places. Daddy thought a lot about politics and the decisions that politicians made in every office from the county judge to the governor and on to the White House. During election season, our whole family went door-to-door campaigning for one politician or another. Daddy was a staunch democrat, but then almost everyone in the state was. There was a short period of time between 1864 and 1874 when republicans ruled the little white house in Little Rock, but other than that, democrats ran the state. Of course, Daddy didn't agree with every democrat. Beginning in 1933, Junius Marion Futrell took office as governor of our great state and Daddy hated that man something fierce.

Futrell didn't like his first name, Junius, so he went by J. Marion Futrell. Daddy called him Junius just to be cantankerous. Months before the election, Daddy started talking up Futrell's opponent. A fat bellied sow pig could have run against Futrell and Daddy would have supported her. According to Daddy, everything that was wrong in the state was on account of Junius. The state was in a horrible mess when Junius took office. Of course the whole country was, so Arkansans weren't alone. Futrell's way of handling the state's deficit was to cut everything. Since he didn't believe that Arkansas really needed educated citizens, he cut funds to schools. This alone would have been enough to anger Daddy. My Granddaddy Baughn died when my daddy was younger than me. Daddy had to quit school after the third grade to help out the family. He was determined that his kids would learn more and do better. "Junius" stood in the way of Daddy's plan.

Daddy loved building roads, and the heavy equipment that made it possible to turn a lung-clogging dirt path into a two-lane highway. His second contention with "Junius" was the governor's answer to the jobless situation. Governor Futrell thought he had a solution to Arkansas' high unemployment. His plan was to get rid of machinery and put the people to work doing manual labor. Daddy told anyone who would listen how stupid this plan was. Even though he had never heard the governor talk, Daddy mimicked him in a high nasally voice, which sounded extra funny coming from his barrel chest. Daddy was a big man, not fat, just tall and imposing.

"Keep 'em stupid and breaking their backs," he would pretend that he was the governor. "No need for us to spend good money on schools. We put all of them uneducated duffuses to work. The fact that they're dead by the time their forty is just a bonus, fewer mouths to feed." Then Daddy would brush his hands together in a snooty way and finish his imitation of Futrell. "Problem solved."

Daddy's third beef against Futrell was his plan to raise money for the state. He gave the okay for gambling in Hot Springs and West Memphis. Daddy didn't have a problem with that. If people wanted to waste hard earned money on the horse or dog races, that was up to them. What he didn't want was the governor's plan to put a tax on Arkansas' liquor. That steamed Daddy something fierce. Prohibition ended in 1933, allowing liquor to once again be sold legally.

In all honesty, we couldn't blame everything on Futrell, but he was the reason that Daddy wasn't at home for my eleventh birthday. When the governor cut the budget, roadwork in Arkansas all but dried up. Daddy was sure that it was personal. After all, he had campaigned against the man hard and heavy, but the truth was that a lot of state employees lost their jobs. Daddy was just one of many. Despite the governor's plan to put men to work instead of machines, a lot of people couldn't find jobs.

The eastern Arkansas Division of the Highway Department practically closed down. The former supervisor of the operation moved to Oklahoma and found work there with the Oklahoma Highway Department. Route 66, which connected Chicago to California covered over 400 miles of Oklahoma roadway. There was always work to be done on it and the many other roads that were being built across the state. When Daddy's former supervisor got settled, he came back for a visit. His first stop was our house. If Daddy wanted to go to work for him, he promised to pay top dollar wages, plus room and board. Daddy jumped at the chance. Every week, he mailed enough money back to Momma to take care of us and pay the rent. There wasn't much cash left over, but we were in better shape than a lot of our friends.

Construction work always has an element of danger to it. Momma worried about what would happen to us if Daddy were injured or killed on the job. During those long nights when Daddy was on a drunk, I dreamed about that very possibility. No more going to bed early and no more bruises for Momma. Maybe she could find another husband, one that would treat her kindly. Sometimes, I felt guilty for thinking such things, but other times, it seemed like a perfect solution to our problems. One time, I made the mistake of mentioning my dream to my older sister, Wanda. She laughed at me and told me that I was stupid. After all, who would want a poor woman with three little girls?

The telephone call surely wasn't about an accident on the job. The sun had set a long time before and even an eleven-year-old kid like me knew it was impossible to lay asphalt after dark. We didn't know what had happened, but from the way Riley Miller was carrying on, it was something terrible bad. Momma told my sisters and me to stay put until she got back, but we followed as she ran across the yard to the Miller's house. The whole Miller family and us girls shamelessly eavesdropped as

Momma picked up the black ear piece that Mrs. Miller had left dangling.

Momma's voice shook as she talked into the mouthpiece. "Hello. Hello. This is Ruby Baughn. Who's this?"

"Bill's been hit by a car. We were pulled over to the side of the road. Bill was changing a flat, and the other driver didn't see him," a metallic female voice answered. She sounded like she was far away and it was hard to make out every word, but all of us could hear what she said. It might have been my imagination, but that woman sounded like she was scared.

Momma wilted into the straight back chair Mrs. Miller had dragged up for her. "How bad is he?" She asked. The shaky voice seemed to be catching, because Momma words quivered as she spoke.

A sob worked its way into the voice of that woman way over in another state. "They think he's broke his back. The driver that hit him took him to the hospital here in Tulsa. They're saying that he'll probably never walk again." Her voice cracked on the last word.

"Exactly who are you?" Momma wanted to know. Everyone else in the room was wondering that the same thing. There was something wrong about that woman calling to tell us what had happened to Daddy. I didn't like that distant voice that brought bad news. It reminded me of a tall blond lady with painted lips and a long cigarette I had seen in a movie.

The silence stretched between the two women on the phone line. The woman sobbed softly. "A friend, just a friend," she finally squeaked. "Bill's calling for you to come."

Momma's face turned from soft to hard in an instant. "You can tell Bill. . . ," Momma started in a high and agitated voice. She stopped midsentence and looked around at all of us stuffed in that little room. Everyone was hanging on her next words. A barely perceptible sigh escaped her. "Tell Bill I'll do my best to figure something out."

Then Momma did something that I had never seen her do before. She behaved rudely. She hung the phone up on that tall, blonde, cigarette-smoking woman and gathered us up. She didn't even thank the Millers for coming to get her or for letting her use their phone. We just left.

As I lay in bed that night, I realized that instead of my dreams coming true, we might be facing my worst nightmare. Not only had Daddy not died, he was coming back to us as a cripple. He couldn't even keep a job now. The months that he had been gone were quiet and peaceful. During the day, we worked in the garden with Momma or helped her take in ironing from the few families who could afford to pay for domestic help. Not once during all those days did we have to go to bed before the sun went down. Ever once in a while, I had even started inviting Martha Sue Carter to spend the night. All of that was over, maybe forever.

My younger sister, Melba, scooted close to me and whispered in my ear. "We're in for it now, aren't we?"

I reached down and took her hand. "Momma always says that tomorrow is a new day," I answered. Neither one of us could have guessed the adventure upon which we were about to embark.

Chapter Two

Moving in with
Grandma and Grandpa

"Melba, don't put the clothes in with the dishes," Momma barked out instructions like a kind hearted general. "We'll need the clothes, but the dishes will stay packed. Jean, be careful with that clock. It belonged to your great grandma Baughn."

Momma could get more done in one day than most people could accomplish in a whole week. Before sunset the day after the phone call, she had talked our great uncle Silas into loaning her a car to go fetch Daddy home when he was able to travel. She called on all of Daddy's friends until she found one that was unemployed and willing to drive uncle Silas' car to Oklahoma. It cost her twenty dollars of hard earned money for gas and expenses, which depleted the last of her emergency funds. Another dollar went to the Millers for two phone calls, one to the hospital to talk to Daddy and the other to Grandma and Grandpa. The bulging sock at the back of her underwear drawer was now completely flat. No more money would be coming in from Daddy any time soon. We had to give up our little rent house next to the Millers and move in with Momma's parents. This was a better option than asking Daddy's momma for help. Grandmother Baughn was an angry old woman who didn't much like kids. Daddy must have gotten his height from her because she towered over all of us, even Momma. It seemed to me that her hands were always perched on her wide hips in a "don't mess with me" pose. Grandma and Grandpa Marshall were nothing at all like her. They welcomed us with open arms.

Grandpa drove his black Ford truck when he came to get us. He pulled into the yard bright and early on a Monday morning, exactly one week after Daddy's accident. We had packed up as much as we could and had it ready to go. Grandpa was a small man, not more than an inch or two taller than Momma, but he was what most people called feisty. There wasn't anything special about his looks, but something about his smile just drew people to him. Grandpa didn't let his size keep him from accomplishing anything. By ten o'clock our belongings were piled high on the old truck and we were packed into that cab like sardines in a can. Momma held my little sister, Melba, on her lap and Wanda sat on me.

"You're tailbone is cutting into me," I complained, but Wanda just wiggled in deeper.

Although Wanda was older and bigger than me, she wouldn't hear of me sitting on her. Her long skinny legs draped over mine like a granddaddy long-legged spider's. When she was just a baby, some neighbor kid tried to pick her up when none of the grown ups were looking. The girl dropped Wanda onto a concrete floor and Wanda had suffered from seizures ever since. It was bad that this happened to my big sister, but it had some unpleasant repercussions for me, too. Nobody, not even Momma or Daddy, ever disciplined Wanda. So most of the time, she was just plain mean to Melba and me. By the time we got to the edge of town, her boney butt had almost worn a hole right through my legs, but I never said a word because Wanda would find a way to make it even worse.

To get to Grandma and Grandpa's house, we had to cross the Black River. Its dark colored waters bisected the fertile farmland. It was less than twenty short miles between the towns of Newport and Newark, but the only way over the Black River was by ferryboat. There was something both thrilling and frightening about riding the ferry. Years ago, a distant cousin of Momma's missed the ferry and drowned in the muddy waters of the Black. Nobody mentioned it as we made our way toward the water, but the story was right there at the edge of our brains.

"There's some good fishing on the river right now. Must be because the water's down some," Grandpa chattered, oblivious to the fear of his passengers. "I bought some channel cat off of Tom Billingsley last week. He said that his trot lines are full every morning. You girls like catfish?" he asked, but we were too scared to answer.

As we approached the steep bank leading down to the river, I grabbed hold of the truck door through the open window. That window was my only way out if the worst happened. Gloomily, I thought of Wanda sitting on my lap, knowing that if we plunged into the river, she would surely trap me and keep me from escaping the underwater tomb. Wanda's torment of me never ended.

Two mules drawing a wagon carefully picked their way down the riverbank in front of us. When they were in place, the ferryman waved us on. My eyes squeezed tight, and I braced myself as I felt the nose of the old truck take a deep dive. The bank was always covered with slick mud, leading right to a strong current, which could sweep us out into the river. In my mind, I could see Grandpa's truck sliding and slipping into the fast-running waters. Several bumps and a clank later, the truck came to a stop. I opened first one eye and then the other to find that we were firmly in place for the crossing. By the time the ferry was full, I had gained a little confidence.

A jolt and a shout and we were off. It took me only seconds to realize that something was horribly wrong. The ferry was not headed to the landing on the opposite side. It was aimed straight at a tall bank up river from the landing.

"Grandpa," I yelled. "We are going to run into the riverbank. We're not going to make it." Instead of squeezing my eyes shut, I now found that it was impossible for me to blink.

A soft chuckle reached me all the way across the cab of the truck. "It just looks that way, Jean. The river current carries us down as we cross, so the ferryman has to aim up high. Let's get out and I'll show you."

Grandpa's door was already opening, and he quickly made his way around to my side of the cab. I was as scared as I had ever been, much more so than when I found out that Daddy had been in a wreck. I didn't want to disappoint this kind old man, so I shuffled Wanda off my lap and gingerly exited the truck.

"Wanda, you and Melba come on too," Grandpa offered. But Melba's arms were locked around Momma's neck and Wanda clung to the dashboard. It was clear that neither one of them were willing to let go, even for a walk with Grandpa.

I probably squeezed every drop of blood out of Grandpa's hand as I clung to him. He didn't complain as he led me over to the rail and pointed to ripples in the water that could have been either fishes or turtles. Before I knew it, the crossing was over. We loaded back up and chugged up the bank on the other side. Grandpa knew the ferryman by name, and yelled, "goodbye Bill," as we left.

"Please Wanda, it's only fair," I begged Wanda to let me sit on her lap when I got back into the truck. Of course, that was a good waste of breath and time. I was once more on the bottom of the stack with her boney butt slicing into my legs like a straight-edged razor. By the end of the ride, I was thinking that Daddy wasn't the only one who couldn't use his legs.

I loved my Grandma and Grandpa Marshall. While Grandpa was short and quiet spoken, Grandma was a tall woman with a personality that was bigger than life. She was waiting for us on the long porch that ran along the whole front of their house. When we rounded the last corner, she ran down the wooden steps and met us before the truck rolled to a stop. She yanked open the door and grabbed Wanda in a bear hug. Grandma Marshall was the one person who didn't bend to Wanda. I loved her even more for that.

"Gracious me, you girls have grown a foot since the last time I saw you," she exclaimed as she put Wanda down with one arm and grabbed me with the other. "Look at you Jean. Your hair is curlier than a pig's tail."

Grandma had a big bosom that was soft and pillowy. She smelled like grape juice, rose petals, and a little hard earned sweat. I wanted to sink into her arms and never come up, but she was already passing me off and reaching for Melba. "Melba and I washed our hair last night and rolled it up in rags," I explained as I touched my curls. "It won't last for long, but I sure do like it."

"Melba, come on and give me a hug," Grandma said, but she didn't wait for Melba to respond before she ripped her off Momma's lap and into her arms. She started talking to Momma, even as she handed Melba down from the truck.

"Ruby, we've got everything ready for you, well, as much as we could. Things are going to be a little cramped around here for a while, but we'll make do." Grandma was already a whirlwind of activity.

Grandpa climbed up into the back of the truck and began to hand down the boxes that held our belongings. Melba and I carried a big box between us while Wanda hefted one box all by herself. My big sister might be mean, but she was strong and not afraid of work. Two hours later, everything was unpacked. The few pieces of furniture we owned were stored in an out building behind the house, and boxes of our clothes were stacked in one of the house's two bedrooms.

Momma insisted that Grandpa move the radio into the front room. My grandparents had a telephone but no radio. Momma said that it was foolish to let ours sit out in the shed when we could be listening to it. If she was in the house during the day, she listened to some show about a woman named Silvia. That poor woman had more hardships than anybody should ever have to go through in one lifetime. Because women mostly listened to those daytime shows while they were doing laundry and ironing, we heard a lot of advertisements from soap companies. Before long, people started calling those programs soap operas. Momma didn't have a chance to listen to daytime radio much in the summer because she was busy gardening outside, but when winter's short, cold days came, she would sit with her quilting and crocheting and cry with poor, poor Silvia.

My sisters and I would rather listen to the Green Hornet. We daydreamed about the handsome Britt Reid as we heard tales of his adventures as a superhero. I felt like the Hornet was telling his story right to me personally as he pulled us into his tale of being a newspaperman by day and a crime fighter by night. Wanda and Melba didn't believe me, but I was sure that I had heard the Green Hornet say that he was the Lone Ranger's grandnephew. Maybe being a superhero ran in family lines. I sure hoped that a taste for liquor didn't run in the blood, because I didn't want to end up like Daddy. Some of the Green Hornet's knockout gas sure would have come in handy on those nights when Daddy had been drinking.

We weren't alone in the house with Grandma and Grandpa. In addition to Momma, Grandma and Grandpa had three other daughters and two sons. All of them were married, except Fenetta. She was born not too long after Momma got married and she was now barely fourteen. It didn't take more than about ten minutes for us to realize that Fenetta didn't really want us there. She had to share her room with all four of us, and she wasn't happy about the turn of events.

"Wanda, you are NOT getting my bed," Fenetta laid down the law. She and Wanda were almost the same age, but Fenetta only came as high as Wanda's shoulders. Her naturally curly hair bounced as Fenetta flounced around the room. "You and the rest of them can sleep on a pallet on the floor. I'm your aunt, and you have to mind me."

Wanda completely ignored her and went about taking over the room. She didn't even listen to Momma, so why should she pay any never mind to a girl who was only a few months older than her, aunt or not.

"Momma," Fenetta yelled to Grandma. "Wanda won't get off my bed. Tell her it's my room and I say what she can and can't do."

Grandma put things in quick order. "Wanda, you will sleep on a pallet on the floor." Fenetta's smirk died on her face when Grandma finished. "All you girls will sleep on the floor. You're young and the floor won't hurt your bones. Ruby will take the bed. When Bill gets here, we'll have to figure out something for him. Right now, the English peas need to be shelled, and there are strawberries to pick if you girls want a cobbler for dessert. Now hop to it, and be careful of wasps when you're picking the berries. They like them as much as we do." And just like that, it was settled. No one argued with Grandma.

We feasted on the best strawberry cobbler in the world. The strawberries were fresh, as were the milk and butter. That night she taught me how to make that mouth watering culinary delight. Grandma called out the ingredients from a cookbook she stored in her head.

"A cup of flour with a pinch of baking soda and salt, a cup of milk, and a cup of sugar. Mix all that together and pour it on top of the melted better. The berries go on top. Add a little extra sugar to the berries before you mix 'em in."

Once it was all cooked together, warm and bubbly, it was the best thing to ever hit my taste buds. When I grew up, I wanted to cook just like Grandma.

We stayed up way past our normal bedtime. It seemed like there were always beans to snap or peas to shell at Grandma's, but it was kind of nice sitting there listening to Momma talk with her parents. Unlike our other grandmother, Grandma and Grandpa Marshall carried on a conversation with us, just like we were regular people and not pesky kids.

"How are you doing in school?" Grandpa directed that question to all three of us.

"Last year, I made four A's and one B," Melba bragged, "and Jean made all A's."

Wanda couldn't wait to show us up. "I'm smarter than both of them. I'm the best reader in the whole school. I've won the spelling bee two years in a row and nobody can beat me at math. I'm smarter than kids three years older than me."

Everything Wanda said was true. She was good at schoolwork. Her problem was people. She just didn't get along with anyone because she was a smart aleck, but we didn't bring this up.

"You must get your brains from your Grandma," Grandpa teased. "She's one smart cookie. You just remember that being smart and pretty are gifts that the Good Lord gave you. He didn't make you do one thing to get them, so don't you get all puffed up with pride. What you do with them, now that's what's important."

"Now Jon," Grandma replied as she playfully elbowed him. "These girls know you're the smart one in the family. And since we're all so smart, we know when it's time to go to bed. Don't we?"

Grandma was right. Our young bodies didn't mind sleeping on a pallet. Spring was almost behind us, and we kicked off the quilts when we first went to bed, but by morning, we were fighting for covers. Wanda and Fenetta argued over who had the most space on their pallet. I could have told Fenetta that she was wasting her breath, but I figured she'd learn soon enough. Wanda was a force to be reckoned with. Melba and I shared a pallet and whispered for a few minutes before we drifted off to sleep. By morning, Fenetta was hanging on to a few inches of bedding, while Wanda took up all the space she wanted. It was the first of many hard lessons for Fenetta that year. Wanda could certainly prepare a body for the disappointments in life.

Over the next few days, we settled into a comfortable routine. Hard work wound down to slow nights. There were no drinking binges or blow-ups, except if you counted Wanda and Fenetta and even they settled into an uneasy truce. In other words, Fenetta learned that she could never win an argument with Wanda. So, she finally quit trying. That didn't keep either one of them from picking on us, so Melba and I avoided them like the Spanish flu. The only cloud on the horizon was knowing that Daddy would be coming back soon. Momma said that he would be able to travel any day now. I wasn't looking forward to that, but there was a bright side. If he couldn't walk, Momma could get away from him easy enough, and he couldn't go anywhere to buy liquor. Grandma and Grandpa didn't keep any spirits in the house, so we didn't have to worry about his temper. When he was sober, Daddy was mostly a good person.

Grandpa and Grandma had apple, pear and peach orchards, a grape vineyard, and a huge garden. They sold some of the produce and dried what fruits they didn't eat during the summer for the winter months to come. Every morning, we laid out big sheets of fabric for drying fruit. Each day we would put the same fruit out on the sheets until it was completely dried up without even a drop of moisture remaining. Come wintertime, Grandma would make tasty dried apple, pear, peach, raisin and plum pies. She was a masterful cook.

Grandpa bought and sold cattle. He purchased herds from area farmers and resold them to packinghouses throughout the area. Grandpa was an educated man, much of it self-taught. He had the skill to buy, sell, and negotiate deals with both the farmers and the businessmen. Grandma was the only midwife in the area, but babies weren't born every day, so she spent most of her time running the family's food enterprises.

Thursday was laundry day at the Marshall house. While Momma, Fenetta and my sisters went down to tend the vineyard and garden, Grandma and I stayed at the house to do the wash. We took turns rubbing the clothes on the rub board and hanging them on the line to dry.

Grandma and I visited as we scrubbed the clothes clean. I separated out the garments that had been stained with grape juice for a special borax treatment while Grandma built a fire under her wash pot. I couldn't wait to use the big paddle to move the clothes around in that boiling pot. Momma wouldn't let me do this chore at home, because she was afraid that an edge of my dress might catch fire. It made me feel grown up that Grandma obviously thought I was big enough for the job.

The road Grandma and Grandpa lived on was a busy one. Several times a day, someone would come by the house to talk business with Grandpa or to ask for Grandma's doctoring advice. So it wasn't a surprise when an old, beat up car pulled into the circle drive. The car might have once been yellow, but it was faded and rusty, making it impossible to know for sure. Dust swirled around a woman and two kids as they got out of the car. Dropping the clothes to soak in the round galvanized tub, Grandma walked out to meet the visitors. The dust blew up again as the car pulled away, leaving the three standing there with as many boxes at their feet.

"Lorene?" Grandma asked, as she hurried toward the woman. "Lorene. Whatever are you doing here? And boys, Clark and Jerry, you've grown a foot since I saw you last," she grabbed one boy and then the other as she talked over their heads to their mother. Apparently, Grandma used this same line on all of us grandkids. We didn't mind because somehow it felt special when she said it to me.

"Lorene, why didn't you write or call to tell us that you were coming for a visit?"

My Aunt Lorene shifted from foot to foot. "Well Momma, we need a place to stay for a while. Jim left me and we don't have any place to go."

Grandma's mouth was a perfect circle, like she was saying "oh," but no words came out. She looked at my mother's sister; I mean really looked. "Oh Lorene, what's happened? I thought you and Jim were so happy."

Aunt Lorene gave a pointed look at the boys. "How about if we talk about it later? We've been stuck in the car for hours and I'm parched. Boys, take your stuff to your Aunt Fenetta's room. I'll get us something to drink."

As Grandma picked up a box and headed toward the house, she glanced over at me. "Jean honey, you keep working on the clothes. I'll be back out to help you in a few minutes."

"What's Jean doing here?" Aunt Lorene asked Grandma as they walked up the steps. "Did Ruby send her for a visit?"

Their voices faded as they entered the house, but I heard Grandma answer just as the screen door slammed closed. Compared to the little house we rented from the Millers, Grandma and Grandpa had a big house. But I had the feeling it had just gotten a lot smaller. Fenetta was going to pitch a fit for sure.

Chapter Three

Grown up Questions

Our sleeping arrangements got shuffled around once again. Aunt Lorene shared Fenetta's bed with Momma, while Fenetta and Wanda continued to battle for space on the pallet in the same room. Clark and Jerry were too little to sleep by themselves, so Melba and I had to move our pallet into the big front room.

"Momma, there's plenty of room in here. Can't we leave our pallet where it is?" I begged.

Melba added her voice to mine. "We'll be quiet as a mouse. You won't even know we're here."

Momma helped Aunt Lorene stack their boxes of clothes next to ours. "Girls, you are sleeping in the front room and that's that!" she said.

We begged every which way to Sunday to get to stay in Fenetta's bedroom. We knew that as soon as Momma and Aunt Lorene went to bed, they would start talking. Melba and I were more than a little bit anxious to find out what happened with Uncle Jim. Daddy didn't like Jim. We also knew that Momma would tell Aunt Lorene things about Daddy that she wouldn't tell us.

When we got too pesky, Grandma laid down the law. "You girls are sleeping in the front room and that's that." Without another word, we moved our blankets without complaint.

I did feel sorry for our poor little cousins. The boys must have gotten their good looks from their Daddy. Jim was quite the looker, but that night, his big blue eyes and pretty white smile held no sparkle. They hadn't said two words all day long. You could tell that they were scared and didn't know what was going on. Jerry started crying as soon as we all got settled in. Clark tried to comfort him, but he was scared too. It didn't take two minutes for Melba and me to move our pallet close to theirs. We told them wild fanciful stories about dragons and castles until they finally fell asleep.

It took another week before Daddy was able to make the trip back to Arkansas. He rode in the back of the car Momma had borrowed from great Uncle Silas. Daddy was still unable to move from the waist down. That woman on the phone was right. He couldn't walk at all. His friend's big muscles strained as he lifted Daddy and settled him into a chair. They were both tanned a leathery brown from working out in the sun, but Daddy looked smaller and more fragile. We expected to have to wait on Daddy hand and foot, but he wouldn't have it. He slipped out of his chair like warm banana pudding and crawled anywhere he wanted to go. Daddy had a lot of bad habits, but being lazy wasn't one of them. Just as soon as he was able, he started helping out with the work.

"Carry my sack down to the garden," he said to Wanda.

Melba and I were still afraid of him, but Wanda reveled in the fact that Daddy couldn't catch her. "Why would you want me to do that? You're not going anywhere."

"You'll do what I say," Daddy barked.

Wanda left the extra sack where it lay and skipped down to the garden, never looking back. Melba grabbed Daddy's tote sack and headed after our sister. He surprised us all when he crawled to the garden on his hands and knees. He held the sack between his teeth as he crawled between the rows and picked the ripe squash.

"Jean," Daddy yelled. "Come and get my sack."

Sweat dripped off Daddy's face and he was trembling all over, but his sack was plum full of squash. Every day, Daddy went to the garden with us. After a time, he didn't seem so exhausted anymore, but he still couldn't walk.

Melba and I were curious to know if Grandma and Grandpa knew about the drinking. We also wondered if Momma had mentioned that woman on the phone to them. If she had, they didn't let on that anything was wrong. They treated Daddy just fine. There was just one time that I thought maybe they knew what happened with Daddy and Momma. Grandpa made a run out to the Barber farm to check some cows. I was mighty tired of working in the garden, so I begged to go with him. I promised to help out and gave my word that I wouldn't get in the way. It didn't take too much effort to get Grandpa to say yes. He loved me extra special.

The cab of the truck was comfortably quiet as we bumped down a winding dirt road. I broke the silence to ask a question that had been plaguing me powerful bad.

"Grandpa, have you ever yelled or hollered at Grandma?" I asked.

He took his eyes off the road for just a second and studied my face. My ears began to warm up under his scrutiny. "I might have raised my voice a time or two, and it could be that I hollered once or twice. Why do you ask, Sugar?"

I turned away from Grandpa's prying eyes as I answered. "No reason, Grandpa. Have you ever hit Grandma?"

"Jean, I want you to listen to me and listen good. The good Lord made a man stronger so that he could protect his family. Protect, Sugar, not harm. There is never a good reason for a man to hit a woman."

"What if he's not at himself, like he's sick or been drinking or something. That's not the same, is it Grandpa?" My eyes were glued to the road as I asked this question.

"Never, Jean, never. A man makes the decision to drink. If he knows that alcohol makes him mean, he ought to stay away from it."

Just about that time, a big tall roadrunner darted out in front of us. I *oohed* and *aahed* over its size, which caused our other conversation to come to a screeching halt. The stupid bird weaved back and forth in front of us before it finally angled off to the side of the road and disappeared into the bushes. I glanced over at Grandpa and noticed a single tear rolling down his check. He never made a move to wipe it off. It just dried right there on his face. I was pretty sure that it was my questions that had made him sad.

The Barber cows were poor and even I could tell they weren't ready for the market. Grandpa suggested that Mr. Barber get some de-wormer and treat the whole herd. Mr. Barber scuffed his already worn out boots against a fence post and didn't say a word.

"I tell you what Charlie," Grandpa said. "I have some extra worm medicine in the truck. If you want to use it, I can take it off the price of the cattle when we sell them this fall. It'll save you a trip into town."

Mr. Barber's whole demeanor changed. His bushy eyebrows wiggled up and down on his forehead like a fuzzy caterpillar when he smiled. It was like a heavy weight had been lifted off his poor bent back. Maybe he'd make something off the sale of those cows after all. Grandpa had just become the answer to his prayers. We visited for a while longer and then headed home.

On the way back, I asked Grandpa all sorts of questions about cows. Grandma might be the one folks called to deliver a baby, but Grandpa knew everything there was to know about cattle. He was very proud of the fact that his son, my uncle Floyd, was away at a school studying to become a veterinarian.

I hoped like crazy that all of the work would be done when we got back to the house, but of course, it wasn't. Momma had killed a chicken, dipped it in boiling water, and had it waiting to be plucked.

She put me right to work. "Jean, I need you to take care of that chicken, while I go get more wood for the cook stove," she said.

I dragged my feet and followed her into the kitchen. "Okay, Momma," I reluctantly accepted the task.

The smell of that scalded bird almost made me sick, but I still pulled the feathers from its puckered skin. The big feathers were hard to pull out, but they covered up more room. It was the tiny little down feathers that were difficult to get. Once I had plucked every feather I could find, Momma was back with the firewood. She found a few spots I had missed and quickly plucked those. Then, she ran the chicken over an open flame on the wood cook stove to singe away any little wisps that we had been unable to remove. After she gutted the bird and cut it up, she put it in a big pan of water. We were having chicken and dumplings tonight. There were so many people in the house now that we had to make the meat stretch as far as we could. We all loved fried chicken, but getting to eat it was a rarity since it would have taken at least two birds to feed us if we prepared it that way.

As the chicken simmered, Melba and I broke the green beans and washed them for dinner. I loved snapping off the twiggy little ends and then dividing the beans into thirds. We had to break out all the bad spots. Most of the time, it was bug bites that marred part of the bean, but sometimes it was because the bean had dragged on the ground and started to rot. Breaking beans was one of my favorite jobs. It was easy work, and I got to visit with Melba. She was my best friend and my only real confidante. Momma had so many problems of her own that I hated to burden her with my worries, but I could share anything with my younger sister. We talked about our hopes and dreams and told each other too many secrets to remember. Sometimes I felt sorry for Wanda. She didn't really have anyone, but then she would do something mean to me and I'd forget all about pitying her.

At the end of the day, Daddy crawled back to the house. Wanda and Fenetta carried his sacks of produce for him. He was plumb worn out, but he didn't complain. Chicken and dumplings, mashed potatoes, green beans with bacon grease, green onions, and cornbread was our supper feast. The meal was delicious, but Daddy didn't eat much. His back was paining him something terrible. Late into the night, he and Grandma sat out on the front porch. They shelled peas or cut up apples, anything to keep their hands busy. Working with his hands helped Daddy keep his mind off the pain. Momma said that Grandma's nerves were bothering her. I couldn't imagine why Grandma would have been having nerve problems. She didn't seem like the nervous type.

Once Clark and Jerry found their voices, we couldn't shut either one of them up. Daddy wanted a boy powerful bad. He was disappointed when Wanda was born and again when he found out I was a girl. By the time Melba came along, he decided that he wasn't going to get a son, so he stuck Melba with a name that would grieve her for years to come. We called my younger sister Melba, but her given name was James Melba. Daddy's name was James William and he was determined to tack his name onto one of his kids, boy or girl. Somehow, Clark found out about Melba's strange first name, and he gave her nothing but misery over it.

"James, James, what a shame, she couldn't get a girly name."

"James, James, what a shame, she couldn't get a girly name."

Those two boys not only taunted her about her name for days on end, they made sure that everyone who came to Grandma and Grandpa's house knew about Melba's dishonor. Wanda didn't much like us, but she didn't cotton to these little interlopers being mean to her sister.

"Cut it out, and I don't mean maybe," Wanda threatened as Clark and Jerry ran a circle around Melba chanting their taunt.

Up to this point, everybody had been walking on eggshells around Aunt Lorene's boys. They were clearly traumatized by the sudden events. No one had mentioned the "D" word, but we knew it was coming. Aunt Lorene was going to be a divorcee. You just didn't see one of those every day. By default, her boys would suffer the shame of her situation, too. Even Wanda had been nice to the little runts, but not anymore. We were out of sympathy. The last drop of it had just run out.

Clark and Jerry learned two things about Wanda. The first was that she was fast, super fast. It was no use trying to run from her, because she could always chase you down. The more you made her work, the worse the punishment. It was better just to take it right away and get over the pain.

The second thing they came to understand was that Wanda never forgot or gave up. One time when I crossed Wanda, she told me that she was going to let me have it. I hid in the bushes out behind the outhouse. There was a deep hole between their branches and it made a perfect place to disappear. For three-and-a-half hours, I sat in that hide-away, waiting for Wanda to forget and go away. Every fifteen minutes, she would come outside and scream at the top of her lungs, "Jean, I'm still here and I will be no matter how long it takes."

At dusk the mosquitoes came out, and the misery of it all finally wore me down. Wanda was true to her word. She was waiting for me as I tried to sneak in through the back door. Not only did she trounce me soundly, one of the mosquito bites got infected and took forever to heal. I learned something then that Clark and

Jerry would soon find out. When it came to Wanda, it was better just to get it over.

Clark ran one way and Jerry the other. For all of her social awkwardness, Wanda was a clever girl. I had read a story about a lioness on the Serengeti in Africa. Just like that magnificent animal, Wanda picked out the youngest, the weakest, and went after that one. His fate was sealed. Once the plan was set into motion, there was nothing Jerry could do to stop it. It took all of ten seconds for her to catch him. Wanda dragged him, kicking and screaming, over to a bucket and stretched him over her lap. Jerry screamed as she spanked him again and again. Tears streamed down his face, and he was unable to stop the sobbing hiccups for what seemed like forever.

Clark had been watching the fate of his little brother from what he thought was a safe distance. When Wanda started walking toward him, he lit out around the house like his britches were on fire. Clark ran as fast as his legs could carry him. His speed was quite impressive, but Wanda was smart, much smarter than a seven-year-old boy. He assumed she would follow him like the person who was "it" in a game of tag, but he was wrong. He glanced back as he ran along the long part of the house on its backside. When he saw no sign of Wanda, he was filled with foolish confidence and slacked up just a little. As he rounded the corner, he ran smack dab into the arms of his tormentor. Wanda had never tried to pursue him. She was smart enough to know that he would circle right back around to her. Since he was older, his whipping was harder than Jerry's, that and the fact that he had had the nerve to think he could best Wanda.

The rest of the day, Melba and I treated Wanda like she was Queen of the Nile. We finished her chores and made sure that she got a little extra dessert at dinner. Even Fenetta was nice to our sister. Wanda had taken care of a job that none of us could do. If we had disciplined the boys, all of the adults would have shamed us something terrible, picking on those poor little unfortunate boys. But Wanda could get away with it. None of the adults, except Grandma, would dare condemn poor Wanda. Not even Aunt Lorene could say anything. What if Wanda got so upset that she had a seizure? I wondered why Grandma didn't say anything. I finally came to the conclusion that Grandma was as tired of the goings on of Jerry and Clark as the rest of us. Discipline by way of Wanda was the perfect solution.

The telephone at Grandma and Grandpa's house didn't ring much. Not many people in Newark had a telephone, so there were few people to call. We kids all got really excited when a call came, but most of the time, it was just the operator checking the line. Grandma said she thought the woman was just bored without enough to do. That night after we went to bed, Aunt Lorene made a rare long distance call.

Chapter Four
A Time of Doctoring and Nursing

As I had drifted off to sleep the night before, I had heard Aunt Lorene whispering into the mouthpiece. Melba and I couldn't make out what she was saying, but I'm pretty sure she was talking to Uncle Jim. After the phone call, she sat out on the back porch for a long time and cried. Her sniffles and hiccups seemed to go on forever. I had felt sorry for Clark and Jerry, but until I overheard that telephone call, I didn't realize how much her husband's abandonment had affected Aunt Lorene.

Our combined families settled in to a comfortable routine. We were three families, but still a part of one bigger, better family. Daddy seemed to be healing some. As long as he had something to hold on to, he could drag himself up and walk a couple of steps. Even though he was still in a lot of pain, he was more patient with us than he had ever been before.

People came from all over to get Grandma's help with their medical problems. Most of them couldn't afford to pay her anything, but they did bring the family all sorts of goods. Just as we were getting ready to go to bed one night, a loud knock came at the front door. A dirty-faced kid about my age stood on the other side of the screened door. He was sweaty and out of breath, like he had run a long way.

"Ms. Ola," he said to Grandma on a heave. "Momma's time is come. Can you come and deliver the baby?"

Grandma was in motion in the blink of an eye. "Come on in Owen, and I'll be ready in a snap. Melba, you run and get my doctoring book, and Jean you help me gather up some clean rags."

In the back corner of Grandma's bedroom, she stored her medical supplies. There was a box with needles of all sizes and some whisker-course black thread. I didn't want to think about how those needles might be used.

"Grandma, why do you need these rags?" I asked, curious about some of the details of her profession, but happily ignorant about others.

She pulled out first one rag and then another. "When a baby is born, you need to make sure that everything is clean. If things aren't clean, infection can set in."

"Won't the family have clean rags of their own?" I asked.

Grandma glanced over at me and whispered like that boy could hear us from all the way out in the front room. "Probably not. The Masons don't believe that cleanliness is next to godliness. Or maybe Mrs. Mason is just too tired. Do you want to go with me and help out? Somebody's going to need to watch the kids, and it wouldn't hurt if somebody straightened up her house a little. I expect it's going to be quit a mess."

Melba heard Grandma's question, just as she entered the room with the doctoring book in her hand. The old volume on the practices of midwifery was tattered and worn from constant use. Grandma had written notes at the edge of many of the fragile pages, and I wondered if the tome would make it through another using.

"I want to go," Melba piped up. My younger sister was normally quiet and rarely asked for a special favor. "When I grow up, I want to be a doctor like you, Grandma."

Grandma looked Melba over good and then it seemed as though she made a decision because the next thing we knew, Melba and I were piling into the truck with Grandma and Owen Mason. Owen smelled like he hadn't had a bath in weeks, which was a good thing. His body odor kind of prepared us for the smell of the house. Grandma was right. This family didn't believe that cleanliness was next to godliness.

The house didn't have a front door, just a tattered cloth covering the opening. Mr. Mason wasn't at home. Owen told us that his daddy was out coon hunting with the boy's uncles, and he didn't know when they would be back. The house was a pigsty. Literally, there was a pig in the front room. Grandma walked right in like she was visiting the governor's mansion. She never said or acted like there was anything wrong with the way the Mason's lived. Melba and I tried to act like her, but it was hard not to gag at the smell. I learned that if I breathed through my mouth, it made it easier to tolerate. After a few minutes, it didn't seem so bad anymore. Mrs. Mason was in the only bedroom of the shack. She called out to Grandma when she heard us come into the house.

"I'll be right in Martha," Grandma replied. "Let me get things settled in here first."

She turned to Owen and talked to him like he was the man of the house. "Owen, I'm going to need your help." Owen's face turned sheet white. He didn't want to have anything to do with helping deliver his next brother or sister.

"But Ms. Ola," he stammered.

"No, no. Not that kind of help. Your daddy's not here and there's going to be a heap of work to do to get ready for this baby. Your momma's not going to feel like doing much work for a couple of weeks. I've brought Jean and Melba to get things in order for her. They're good workers, but they're not strong enough to carry water or move heavy stuff. I'll depend on you to do that." And just like that, Grandma had gotten us all the help we needed and made Owen feel important at the same time. Grandma had a gift that way.

Besides Owen, the Mason's had two other kids. The youngest one looked to be between one and two. The red hair must have run in the family, because his red mop looked just like Owen's. The baby's diaper was black dirty and it was so wet it was sagging to his knees. I had a weak spot for little kids and it plum near broke my heart to see those children in that shape. Melba and I would do all we could to put their house in order while Grandma delivered the baby. I guessed the first order of business was to get the pig out of the house.

Owen and I had a bit of a tussle over that. He thought the pig was just fine as an inside pet. Sadly, it was probably the cleanest thing in the whole house, but everything in me said that it had to go. We finally reached a compromise. Owen agreed to find another place for the pig until I got the front room and the kids cleaned up. Melba and I didn't know what to do first, work on the house or the kids. If we cleaned the kids before the house, they would just get dirty again. We finally decided to change the baby and then work on the house. The baby had a rash on his butt that was raw and red.

Owen carried bucket after bucket of water for us and never once complained. I wonder if he was ashamed of the way his family lived and wanted something better. He was nice and mannerly, and we would have never gotten that room even moderately clean without his help. Once the floor was swept, the dishes washed, and every surface mopped down with a wet rag, it was time to start in on the kids.

Owen filled an old number three washtub full of water, and I hunted until I found some lye soap for their baths. Grandma called for one of us to come and help her for a minute, and Melba jumped at the chance. Little Freddy was almost asleep when I sat him into the tepid bath. Thank goodness it was warm outside, and we didn't need to build a fire to heat up the water. Bless his little heart, he cried when his raw little bottom hit the water. Although it was hard to do, I ignored his cries and gave him a good, thorough washing. When I finished, I peeked into the bedroom to ask Grandma about using one of the clean rags for a diaper. Melba told her about the diaper rash, and she had a bit of doctoring advice for it.

"Sprinkle a little bit of flour or corn starch on the rash before you put the rag on him. It would be better if you could scorch it on the stove first, but it's too hot in here to heat up the stove."

Owen carried in more water while I diapered Little Freddy and got him ready for bed. I hated to put that sweet smelling little boy down on the dirty pile quilts that made up his bed. Unfortunately, the Mason's didn't have anything else and I didn't have time to wash all the bedding and have it dry.

Milton Mason was next. He looked to be about Clark's age, maybe six or seven. He wasn't real excited about getting a bath, but when Owen laid down the law, Milton didn't complain too much. He didn't want me to help with the washing, but I was afraid that he would just take a dip in the water if I didn't supervise. Owen and I scrubbed his head, behind his ears, and his neck. We also took a soapy cloth to his hands and feet. We left everything in between for him to wash by himself. Chances are that those parts didn't get a good cleaning, but he was old enough to take care of those things that should be private. I turned my back when he got out of the tub. We must have done some good because a thick layer of grayish brown scum floated on the surface of the water.

Not long before dawn, the latest Mason came into the world. She had curly red hair and was as fat as a little piglet. Mrs. Mason was happy to have a girl at last. She laughed and thanked Grandma like she was the one who decided that the baby would be a girl. She named the baby Petunia, which sounded a little like a pig name to me. I didn't renege on my promise to Owen, so the real pig was brought back into the house. When we left, the yearling was snuggled down between the two little boys sound asleep. Melba and I dozed off on the way home. Much to the frustration of Wanda and Fenetta, we got most of the following day off from doing any chores. Every time they came near the house, they made as much noise as was humanly possible. We didn't get much sleep, but we didn't let on to them that they were bothering us. That would have given them too much satisfaction.

Late that afternoon, Mr. Mason showed up with a deer as payment for Grandma's hard work. After he left, Daddy checked to make sure it had been freshly killed before we set about butchering it. This was something Daddy did real well. After tying a rope around the front hooves and pulling it up onto the branch of a tree, he set about skinning it. His back still wouldn't allow him to stand for long, so he and Grandpa worked on it together. Just as soon as they had the tenderloin cut out from along the backbone, Melba and I rushed it to the house. We had to get it into salt water if we were going to have it for supper. While the tasty tenderloin soaked, Daddy taught me how to cut up a deer. He showed me how to separate the meat from the joints and tendons and pointed out the lymph nodes that needed to be cut out. The hams and steak were put in the smoke house to cure. This process would keep the meat from ruining for weeks. Some of the smaller, scrappier parts were seasoned and set out to dry for jerky.

Melba and I helped Momma and Aunt Lorene tenderize the tenderloin. Using the edge of a tin can, we pounded the meat until it was practically falling apart. Then Momma dusted it with seasoned flour and slowly fried it in bacon grease. When Momma was finished cooking the meat, she took the bits of flour and meat that were left in the skillet and made white gravy. Grandma scraped together just enough okra and two nearly ripe tomatoes to make the meal perfect. It was her first mess of okra for the year and it tasted almost as good as the venison. I ate so much for supper that I ended up with a bellyache. Grandma gave me a pinch of baking soda and a glass of water to settle my stomach. Grandma's patients might not have been able to give her cash money, but my belly sure liked their creative methods of payment. As we would soon learn, not all of their gifts were so welcome.

Chapter Five
The Bonus Gift from the Masons

Grandma and Grandpa were God loving, God fearing people. There was never a question about what the family would be doing on Sunday morning. The Mount Olive Presbyterian church almost doubled in size the year our family and Aunt Lorene's moved in with my grandparents. The women got up extra early on Sunday morning to pick the vegetables and cook Sunday dinner. The men all talked about Sunday being a day of rest, but there was never a day of rest for the women.

The whole family took baths on Saturday night. If Melba and I had enough time, we wrapped our hair in rags to get those soft curls that Grandma so admired. If we didn't have time, we French braided our hair on Sunday morning. Wanda wore her hair in a short bob and Momma always helped her finger curl it before church. As she combed Wanda's hair and worked to create a stylish ridge along the top, Momma discovered a horrible secret hiding in those silky brown tresses. Somehow, somewhere, Wanda had come in contact with head lice. There weren't that many adult lice on her head, but the lice had done a good job of attaching their eggs to dozens of strands of hair. Those nits shimmered a silvery color against Wanda's dark hair. Panic ensued as each and every head in the family was checked. Only Grandpa, who was near bald, was free of these parasitic insects. Grandma sent him on to church but made him promise that he wouldn't tell the congregation the reason the rest of us were absent. Everybody at church knew there must be a good reason for us to miss. Grandpa told them that we were all in bed with the runs - well between the bed and the outhouse. When several of the women offered to come help with the work, he improvised and told them that Grandma hadn't been affected. Grandpa pure dee hated lying, and lying in the church bothered him double. It was like a twofold insult to God.

While the good saints were singing and worshipping, we were taking turns picking those little varmints out of our hair. I picked on Melba for a while and when my fingers wore out and her neck got tired, we switched around. Jerry cried and begged to be left alone, but Aunt Lorene swatted his bottom and made him sit still. Wanda was convinced that Melba and I had brought these bugs home from the Mason's, and Grandma didn't disagree with her. If a pig was the cleanest animal in the house, living with head lice probably wasn't a big concern for the Mason family.

Fenetta had a way of asking questions that seemed to always get Melba and me into trouble. "Momma, don't you think that Jean and Melba should be punished for bringing these lice to us? We had to miss worship and everything." She conveniently left out the fact that Grandma went to the Masons too, and that Grandma was the one who asked both of us to go with her.

"Fenetta," Grandma said in a long suffering sigh. She sounded out Fenetta's name like it had ten syllables. Maybe she felt sorry for her youngest daughter since all of us moving in had upset her life, but she almost never got on to her, not even when Fenetta was outright mean to us.

"I'm just saying that if I had brought something like this home, I would expect to be held accountable for it." Fenetta tried one last time to get us in trouble.

Momma knew we were interlopers here in her parent's house, so she rarely made any waves when it came to Fenetta's pettiness. But there is a point that every mother reaches when her children have to be defended. Momma had reached that place.

"Who's to say that the girls are the ones who brought in the lice, Fenetta? Maybe it was the young man I've seen you sparking with. Your head was close enough to his for lice to crawl from his head to yours."

Fenetta was masterful at deflecting blame. She wasn't old enough to spark with a boy and everybody knew it. She completely ignored what Momma said about the boy, and turned on her instead. She jumped to her feet and planted her hands on her hips. Her cheeks were rosy red with anger, and from her vantage point she towered over mother. "How dare you come into MY house and accuse ME of such a thing?"

Momma had made her point. She didn't even look at her spoiled younger sister.

"Mommmaaaaaaaa," Fenetta whined. "Are you going to let her talk to me like that?"

"Feeennnnetta," Grandma replied, like somehow that said everything she needed to hear.

Fenetta stormed out of the room but came back in a few minutes to have Grandma finish picking her hair. She was angry, but she wasn't stupid. If she went off on her own, she would still have lice. Her curly blonde hair was Fenetta's best feature. The thought of those bloodsuckers living on her scalp helped Fenetta to get her priorities in order.

For days, Momma would spot check our heads. Occasionally she would find another nit, but eventually, we got rid of every last louse in our house. Doing away with them for good took a lot of extra work on our part. Every sheet, pillowcase and quilt had to be washed. Laundry day came twice that week. By Saturday, we were plum tuckered out, and the adults gave us the afternoon off to play.

Fenetta found a book and sat down under a shade tree to read. The boys went down to the creek to catch crawdads and pollywogs. Melba and I made a playhouse.

We found a spot of sandy ground, which we swept clean – or as clean as you can sweep dirt. Our four-room house was divided with rocks we carried from the edge of the yard. Melba found an old tin can to use as a vase for the brown-eyed susans and yellow bitter weeds we picked for a bouquet. It adorned the center of the floor in the room we designated as our kitchen and dining room. Just across the road from Grandma's house, there was a bank of red, clay mud, characteristic of Arkansas soil, that made the best pottery plates and glasses in the world. Melba and I spent hours sculpting that mud into dishes for our playhouse. After we were finished making our dishes, we rolled them in salt to give them a sparkle and sat them on our "back porch" to dry. We pretend ironed, cooked pretend food, fed pretend babies, and kissed pretend husbands before sending them off to pretend jobs. It never struck us as strange that we were pretending to do most of the things we called chores in our day-to-day lives.

Wanda was the odd kid out. Without work, she didn't know what to do with herself except irritate everyone else. She shook the tree Fenetta sat underneath until she was showered with leaves. Jerry and Clark were scared out of their britches when she snuck down to the creek and made animal noises in the weeds. They came screaming back to the house and we never did convince them that it was just Wanda playing a joke. When they went down to the vineyard to find their momma, Wanda finally found her way to our "house." She walked straight through the walls, ignoring our clearly marked doorways.

After that, she squished our dishes and threw out our bouquet of flowers. According to her, they were just stinking weeds. By dinnertime, we were ready for chores again. Given the choice of working or playing with Wanda, Melba and I would always choose work.

That next day at church, we were surrounded by friends who wanted to make sure we were feeling better from our stomach upset. Wanda let the cat out of the bag and announced to everyone within hearing distance that we hadn't been sick at all. Then she proceeded to tell anyone who would listen that we had gotten head lice. Wanda was very precise in her speech. Each word was clearly enunciated and she put emphasis on special words that helped the listener read between the lines.

"We don't know for sure," she announced to the horrified listeners. "They miiiight have come from the Mason family. Grandma went out to deliver their baby. Ooooor, it could have been Fenetta's caller. He's been hanging around the house and Fenetta could have brought them in from him. Since she had the most, I think that may be the source."

A stunned silence followed her announcement. As usual, Wanda seemed totally oblivious to the magnitude of the trouble she had caused. Grandpa was ashamed of being caught in a lie. Grandma was embarrassed that her friends knew about the family's trouble with head lice, but that was nothing compared to Fenetta's mortification. Her mouth gaped open wide and she slowly shook her head "no" as she looked behind her to the back of the church. A tall, handsome boy sat on the very last pew. It wasn't just his good looks that sat him apart. It was the blood-red embarrassment that stained his checks.

"Wanda Lee Baughn!" Grandma said. Huh oh, Wanda had gotten the full name treatment. That always meant trouble.

"What?" Wanda asked with all innocence. "I do think it was Fenetta's boyfriend. You wouldn't want me to lie would you?"

Grandma got real quiet. No doubt, her nerves would be bothering her tonight. Momma sat beside me on the pew. Her head was down and her whole body was shaking. Wanda had finally done it. She had embarrassed Momma to tears. I put my hand in hers and gently squeezed. It was only when she glanced at me that I realized it was not tears that shook her little frame. It was laughter. Her wink told me to keep her secret. After all, it wouldn't seem very ladylike to find such pleasure in Fenetta's humiliation. Once again, Wanda had carried out the family discipline, and no one could do anything about it.

The walk back home was carried out in near silence. Fenetta sobbed longer and harder than Jerry had when Wanda spanked him. Seemingly oblivious to the trouble she had caused, Wanda skipped and joked with the boys. Since she didn't have any friends, she didn't worry about losing anyone's respect. Fenetta would have cried even louder if she had known that she had more trouble on the way.

Chapter Six

Fireworks in the Outhouse

As we entered the month of July, the days got hotter and hotter, with a stifling humidity that made each day miserable. Some nights the heat made it impossible for us to sleep. Daddy had settled into a day bed out on the back porch. The heat was hardest on him. According to the radio, we were in the middle of a heat wave. There were record-setting temperatures even in the northern states like Michigan, Wisconsin, and Indiana. One afternoon, the adults took pity on us and let us go down to the creek to cool off. We didn't have bathing suits, so we all wore cutoff britches. The boys didn't have to wear shirts, but the girls borrowed grandpa's tee shirts for covers on top. I was not a good swimmer and wouldn't get out in the waters that were over my head, but Wanda and Melba swam like fish. Fenetta was still sulled up over the incident at church and floated on top of the water down stream from the rest of us.

Aunt Lorene and Momma came down for a little while, taking care to watch after the boys. They sat on the bank and talked while we splashed each other in the water. I heard bits and pieces of their conversation and finally figured out what had happened to Aunt Lorene's marriage.

Back in those days, dirty words weren't heard every day. If a kid was heard saying a dirty word, she was likely to get her mouth washed out with soap. I know this from experience since I said the "S" word one time and had to take a bite out of a flowery scented washing bar. Palmolive soap's Cashmere Bouquet didn't taste so flowery in my mouth, and I never said that word again. Occasionally, we heard a man say a dirty word, but that usually happened when he didn't know that kids or women were within hearing distance. It was rare indeed for a woman to cuss. But that day, as I eves dropped from the creek, I heard Aunt Lorene say a word that to our family was the worst of the worst. She used the "L" word, which was far worse than the one I said.

"I love him something terrible, but he's *lazy*,' Aunt Lorene explained at least part of the reason her marriage was ending. "The boys and I could starve for all he cares. He just won't get out and get a job -- won't even try. Besides, I think there's another woman."

There must have been something powerful persuasive about Uncle Jim, because Aunt Lorene was his forth wife. If he was lazy, I couldn't help but wonder what it was about him that made a woman want to take a chance on him. If you were real old, like I thought my mother and her sister were, he might have been kind of handsome, but I wasn't real impressed.

Aunt Lorene lowered her voice, which made it more difficult for me to hear every word. I had to listen mighty hard. "Jim doesn't ever go see his other kids. I can't help but worry that he'll completely forget about Clark and Jerry."

From the corner of my eye, I thought I could see her wiping a tear or two, but I didn't want her to know that I was listening in, so I didn't look right at her. I could see Momma put her arm around her sister. You could read the sympathy in Momma's every move. I wondered if Momma wished that she could muster up the courage to leave Daddy. Her life with him wasn't easy. They talked on quietly a few minutes before deciding that Clark and Jerry were fine and headed back to the house.

In our family, laziness was just not tolerated. Daddy's drinking was more acceptable than a lazy man would have been. The Bible says that a man who won't feed his family is worse than someone who doesn't even believe in God. Daddy wasn't a God fearing man, but even he understood this basic principle of life. I glanced over at poor little Clark and Jerry and hoped that laziness wasn't hereditary. It would sure be a shame if they grew up to be good for nothing bums.

On the way back to the house, we crossed through a field that was filled with prickly pears. A lot of flowers had dried up in the summer heat, but those cacti that grew close to the ground were in full bloom. Their fluffy yellow blossoms transformed the ground into a beautiful garden. From the time that I was Jerry's age, I had loved flowers. No matter where we lived, I found a way to plant a flower garden.

"Fenetta, what kind of flowers are those?" I asked.

She came out of her sulk to answer me and to my surprise, she seemed quite helpful and informative. "Why those are blooming pear plants."

"They sure would make a pretty flower bed. Don't you think?"

"Of course, they would. You should carry some of them back to the house. Momma would love to have a flower garden out front of the house."

I didn't need any extra encouragement. I waded out into the field and gently dug up those "blooming pears." Wanting to get a full garden, I stacked plant after plant into my arms. By the time I got to the house, my arms had started to itch and sting. When I gently placed the plants down, I discovered that those showy yellow plants had tiny little stickers on every plump leaf. As I had carried them to the house, hundreds of those hair-fine stickers had become embedded in my arms. When I tried to pick them out, they broke off even with the skin.

Fenetta just stood there and watched me with a possum eating grin on her face.

As the realization of my situation sunk in, I started to cry. "Momma," I screamed. "Help me."

Everybody came running. Momma was expecting something horrible bad because I almost never cried. Living with Wanda kind of toughened a body up that way. When I showed her my arm, she sucked in a deep breath. "Jean, how did this happen?"

I told them how I had seen the flowers and wanted to plant some close to the house. With hands on her hips, Grandma turned to Fenetta.

"Fenetta, why didn't you warn her?" Grandma wanted to know. For the first time in the long weeks since we moved in, Grandma lost her patience with Fenetta. She might have been more tolerant if she had played such a trick on Wanda considering their on-going feud. But I had never crossed Fenetta. For the next week, Fenetta was made to do all of the least desirable chores. She paid for her mischief, but the worst of her repayment was still to come.

Grandma got her doctoring supplies and went to work on my arm. We carried chairs out into the yard to catch the best light and she gently removed those fragile little needles. After hours of work, she had barely made a dent in the number. She found a recipe in one of her doctoring books for a drawing poultice. Once she mixed it up, she gently spread it over my arm and then covered with strips of clean rags. I hoped that by morning time, the poultice would draw those little buggers out, but I was in for a disappointment. Momma and Grandma took turns working on my arms. If felt like the stickers had poison on them, because my skin swelled up and started to itch something miserable. By the end of the week, it was some better, but Grandma insisted I keep the rag bandages on to keep out infection.

As the forth of July approached, Grandma and Grandpa invited friends and neighbors to a potluck dinner. If the weather cooperated, we'd eat outside, making it a true dinner on the grounds. The day before, Grandma sent Melba and me over to old Mrs. Estes' house to help make pies. She was short, like Momma, but Mrs. Estes wasn't nearly so padded. Her skinny hands reminded me of the talons of a bird of prey. Her rock house was built so that the kitchen was separated from the main house by a deep breezeway. It was still hot in the kitchen, but at least it kept the rest of the house from heating up too.

We took enough blueberries for two pies. The night before grandma put some dried apples in water to soak. There were enough of those apples for two more pies, and finally, the last two pies were my personal favorite. Buttermilk pie may not sound very tasty, but I'm here to tell you that it is pure dee delicious. When you mix that clotted milk with eggs, sugar, and a little bit of vanilla flavoring, it makes a mouth-watering treat. The only bad thing about fixing all those pies was waiting to eat them. We promised Mrs. Estes to come over bright and early the next morning to help her carry the pies to the social. When we got there, one of the pies was gone. Mrs. Estes said that a mouse had gotten in to it, but Melba and I decided that she just hadn't been able to resist digging into one of them. We didn't blame her too much. After all, she had been alone with them overnight, and put in the same situation we might have done the same thing.

Independence Day turned out to be hotter than a firecracker. Grandpa pulled a couple of flatbed wagons around to the front yard. Wanda spread long clothes over the wagons in preparation for the food. She brushed all of the dirt off of a few rocks and put those on top of the clothes to keep them from blowing away. Momma and Aunt Lorene went down to the garden and came back with a bushel full of corn. We kids shucked it, and Daddy took a knife to all of the worm holes. He tossed any worms that were still in the ear into a can. They would make good bait for fishing later. We would boil the corn right before we ate. It didn't take but just a few minutes for corn on the cob to cook.

About mid morning, people started to show up. Most of them arrived by wagon, but a few walked. Not many people had a motor vehicle. Every family raised a garden, so we had all kinds of vegetables prepared every way that you could imagine. There were five different kinds of squash alone, including a fabulous tasting relish. We didn't fix breakfast what with all the preparation needed for the potluck. By lunchtime, my mouth was watering up a storm. Momma gently swatted my hand when I tried to sneak a piece of fried chicken.

Everybody was surprised when the Mason family showed up. According to Grandma, they mostly associated with family and never came to things like this. She reminded us to be nice to them, even if they had given us head lice. "We don't know for sure that they gave it to us, but just to be on the safe side, we'll just wash our hair in mint water before we go to bed tonight." I couldn't understand why lice would dislike the smell of mint. It smelled fabulous to me.

Owen and the two other boys were all cleaned up, and even baby Petunia looked like she had had a good bath. I paid close attention to the food they brought, because I didn't think they were probably clean in their cooking. I whispered that information to Melba and Wanda, but I didn't tell Fenetta. She was still on my bad side for playing that trick on me with the prickly pears. My arms were still sore and bandaged.

Melba and I ooohed and aaahed over the Mason's new baby. Like the rest of the Mason kids, she had curly red hair about the color of a new copper penny and pale white skin. The coloring looked better on her than it did on the boys. Mrs. Mason looked plumb tuckered out, so we volunteered to sit on a pallet with the baby while she visited. Owen talked with the boys for a while and then wondered over to the pallet on the pretense of keeping an eye on the baby. When he went to get cold drinks for us, Melba whispered to me that she thought he was struck on me. I didn't disagree with her, because he was sure paying me plenty of attention.

As I reached out to take the drink from Owen, he noticed my bandages. "What happened to your arms?" he asked.

Melba and I told him how Fenetta had tricked me into picking both arms full of prickly pears. His fair complexion turned bright red with anger. "That was a nasty prank," he said when we finished our tale.

"She doesn't like it that we're here," Melba explained. "She's been mean to us all summer long."

We talked about that a little bit longer when Owen noticed a snake sunning itself on a rock not far from our pallet. It scared Melba and me, but Owen reassured us that it was just a garter snake and wouldn't hurt a flea. "Leave it be," he said, "and it'll leave you be."

Fenetta was flirting with that handsome boy from church. I guess she had reassured him that she was free of head lice. She giggled and batted her eyes like a perfect ninny. After a few minutes, she sauntered away from her beau and stopped by our pallet on her way to the outhouse.

"Do you have a little boyfriend, Jean?" she asked in her snotty way. "If I were you, I'd be careful of getting too close if you know what I mean."

Fenetta knew better than to bring up the head lice incident directly. Neither Grandma nor Grandpa tolerated any of us treating others badly. Poor Owen's face turned bright red, and one of his hands clinched into a tight fist.

We knew how he felt and wondered if word had gotten back to him about what Wanda said at church. I hoped that he hadn't heard about it, because he seemed like a nice boy and I didn't want to hurt his feelings. From the look on his face I could tell that he wanted to sock Fenetta something fierce, but he was powerless to do so.

The outhouse was situated behind the house. Once Fenetta was inside, Owen didn't say a word. He just walked over and picked up that snake we had been watching. He disappeared around the side of the house, and it didn't take us long to figure out what he was up to. Fenetta's scream was loud enough for everybody at the picnic to hear.

A few seconds later, Fenetta tore around the house like she was being chased by a rabid hound. "Mooooooommmmmmmaaaaa," she wailed as she pointed to us. "They threw a snake in the outhouse with me. They tried to kill me."

Melba and I sat on the pallet, the perfect picture of innocence painted on our faces. "We were here taking care of the baby," I said. We had at least two dozen witnesses, so nobody could put the blame on us.

Fenetta searched the crowd trying to figure out who had done this horrible thing. Mason blended in with the men, and she completely overlooked him. "I know they had something to do with this. They hate me," she screamed. She was right, but we didn't volunteer that information.

"Girls, do you know anything about this?" Grandma questioned.

We shook our heads and lied through our teeth. "No, Grandma, we didn't see anything."

Grandma searched our faces for the truth. "You know that someone could have been hurt."

Melba was normally the sweetest and kindest of all of us. She rarely talked back or sassed our elders. When she did, that adult was always left wondering if she was being smart mouthed or not. This was one of those times. "Don't worry, Grandma. I think the snake will probably be okay."

With no clear person to blame, Fenetta fell into a frustrated sob. She cried and cried. Her beau didn't seem to know what to do. She obviously wanted his sympathy, but even he thought it was kind of funny. I'm not sure whether Fenetta went to the outhouse to do number one or number two, but I'm pretty sure that once that snake hit her, she did all of the numbers. It was the best Fourth of July ever. We didn't even need firecrackers to see the sparks fly.

Chapter Seven

Tighter than Bark on a Tree

After the exciting picnic, Grandma and Grandpa decided to take a little trip to visit Aunt Violinia. She was Momma's older sister. Her family lived in Augusta, which seemed like a world away from Newark to me. When she was just fourteen, Aunt Violinia ran off and married a farmer down in the bottomland. They had a passel of kids. From what Momma said, they were dirt poor and rarely came to visit. The few times I had seen them, Melba and I got along with those cousins really well. They were nice and polite, and more importantly, they were hard workers.

We decided that Grandma and Grandpa needed to get away from their overstuffed house, or maybe they wanted to give Fenetta a break after the incident in the outhouse. Either way, we were as excited to see the backside of Fenetta as she was to go. They headed out bright and early the day after the fourth.

That night, we helped Momma fix dinner while Aunt Lorene cleaned house and supervised the boys' bath. Since there were fewer of us at the house, the women planned a rare treat of fried chicken. Wanda was so anxious to eat the liver that Momma put her in charge of cooking the chicken. As she stood next to the stove with fork in hand, Wanda's eyes glazed over, and her hand dropped into the hot grease. Momma was dusting the okra in corn meal when she realized what was happening.

Momma yanked Wanda's hand out of the frying pan and screamed for Daddy. He was walking more and more every day and came into the kitchen as fast as he could. Between the two of them, they carried Wanda into the front room and laid her down on the sofa.

"Jean, get some cold water," Daddy yelled. I had been watching what was happening in a frightened stupor. Suddenly, I was in motion, chipping chunks of ice from the block in the ice box and filling a pan of water that Melba had ready. We rushed into the front room and handed the water to Momma.

Tears rolled down Momma's checks as she gently placed Wanda's hand in the cool water. Melba and I held on to each other and cried too. Wanda's seizures were a part of our lives. We had never known anything different, but it was still scary. Grandma had explained to us that there were all kinds of seizures. Wanda didn't have the fall down twitching kind. It was just like she went to another place, and her body was no longer under her control.

Melba and I moved to the top of the couch and gently combed Wanda's hair with our fingers. Slowly, she came out of the stupor and looked around. I bent down and gently kissed her forehead. "You had a seizure, but it's going to be okay," I reassured her. The pain was setting in, and she started to cry. For the first time, I understood why Momma and Daddy gave over to Wanda. This was a horrible thorn in the flesh to live with. Aunt Lorene and the boys stood at the edge of the room. The boys didn't understand exactly what was going on, but they knew something was wrong. They clung to their momma's skirt, and Jerry started to cry with all of us.

Aunt Lorene finished dinner and set the table for us to eat. None of us were very hungry after that, so the fact that the chicken was burned didn't much matter. Melba got Grandma's doctoring book and read up on burns and how to treat them. Then she rummaged through grandma's medical corner and found some supplies. The book said to put melted butter on the burn, but Momma didn't agree with that. They just continued to soak it in cool water and when Wanda could stand it, Momma put one of Grandma's special salves on it. Before bedtime, she wrapped it in a clean white cloth. Momma and Daddy sat up with Wanda all night long. Wanda and Fenetta's pallet was empty, but Melba and I still slept together. Somehow we didn't want to be alone tonight.

A few days later, things were almost back to normal. We looked at Wanda's hand everyday when Momma changed the bandage. Several sores covered her fingers and palm and oozed a milky liquid. Momma wanted Grandma to come home soon to make sure that Wanda's hand was going to be okay. We didn't know exactly how long they were going to be gone.

We still had daily visitors. Word hadn't gotten around that Grandma and Grandpa were out of town, and folks stopped by to talk to them. Momma and Aunt Lorene knew most every visitor. The Pricherts lived down the road a piece. Mrs. Prichert and Aunt Lorene had gone to school together, but our aunt didn't seem real excited to see her old classmate. She had two boys that were about the age of Melba and me, but they were quiet a bit bigger than us and a whole lot meaner. They were with their momma one afternoon when she stopped by to borrow some milk. Grandma complained that Mrs. Pritchert was always running out of something. Grandpa said that it was just her way of saving on the grocery bill. One of the boys, I think it was Milton, noticed Wanda's hand. He sidled up to me and asked what happened to her.

"She sometimes has seizures," I started to explain.

That smart allecky Prichert boy got a smirk on his face that I didn't much like. "You mean like a mad dog?"

Once again, I tried to explain, but he wasn't listening. "Your sister's just like a mad dog. Does she foam at the mouth?"

Suddenly, a rage like nothing I had ever felt before filled every inch of my body. Before I knew what was happening, I jumped on that big ole boy and wrestled him to the ground. My fingernails dug into his face, and I racked them down to his chin. I didn't stop there. Next I grabbed his hair and pulled with all of my might. Clumps of his brown tresses came out in my hands. While I worked on the top half, Melba worked on the bottom. She kicked his legs with all her might.

I'm not sure what would have happened to him if Momma hadn't pulled us off of him. "Girls," she screamed. "Stop it this instant."

Mrs. Prichert came running when she heard her boy yelp. When she saw the things we had done to Milton, she lit into to Momma like an angry she bear. "What kind of girls are you raising? Just look at what they've done to my poor little Milton."

She examined him from head to foot. The marks on his face were the worst. It would take weeks for those to heal. Momma didn't offer her any special suave. "I expect you to do something about this. Those girls have to be punished, and I don't mean with the palm of your hand."

Daddy stepped out onto the porch. He had been listening to the goings on from inside the house. "Don't worry Mrs. Pritchert," he said as he removed his belt. "We'll make sure the girls are punished. Girls, get in the house."

I don't know if it was the after effect of the beating I had given Milton or the fear of Daddy whipping me with a belt, but my knees were knocking together and my lower lip trembled as I walked up the wooden steps. Melba raced up beside me and put her hand in mine. No matter what Daddy did to us, I wouldn't apologize. That Pritchert boy had it coming to him.

Momma and Daddy followed us into the house. "Bill," Momma began. "You aren't going to belt them, are you?"

Daddy motioned his head outside and lowered his voice. "I'd bet ten bucks that Pritchert woman is still out there listening. When I hit, y'all be sure and let out some good screams."

Melba and I suddenly realized that were we not in trouble after all. Daddy swung his belt and it sank deep into the soft couch. I screamed at the top of my lungs. "Daddy don't hit me," Yelling in what I thought was a pretty convincing way, Melba and I let out one yelp after another. Daddy whipped that couch two ways from Sunday while Melba and I put on a show of pain. Mrs. Pritchert finally left the yard, satisfied that we had gotten what we deserved.

Wanda was still outside, and Momma called her in. We told her the trick Daddy had played on the Pritchert's. She smiled but never really said anything. Seeing Wanda sad made me mad all over again. If Milton Pritchert had showed up in our yard, I might have lit into him again.

That night after super, we sat on the front porch and listened to Daddy talk about Oklahoma. Daddy drew us a map so that we could see where Oklahoma was. It was clear on the other side of the state, but it seemed so far away that it might as well have been a foreign country. All of the sites sounded so distant and exotic. The farms in Oklahoma had dried up, and much of the dirt had blown away. We listened, hanging on to each word as Daddy told us about getting caught in one of those dust clouds.

"We were out working on the road. I was up on top of one of the big rigs when one of the boys spotted a big brown cloud on the horizon. Oklahoma isn't hilly like Arkansas. It's mainly flat, and you can see out for miles in all directions."

He held us enthralled in the spell of his story. "What was it?" Little Jerry asked.

"At first, we didn't know. We thought it might be a storm, but it was a color I had never seen in the sky. There was this old Okie fellow working out in his field. He came running toward us, screaming that we had to take cover. That storm blew in before we knew what happened."

"Was it a tornado?" Melba eagerly asked. "Were you in the middle of a twister?" We were familiar with storms, especially tornados. Back in April, we had heard on the radio about a killer tornado hitting first Tupelo, Mississippi and then later Gainesville, Georgia. In two days time, that storm had killed over 400 people. As Daddy described the site, I envisioned a big, dark thunderhead.

Daddy shook his head at Melba's question. "Nope, it wasn't a tornado. It was a wall as tall and as wide as the sky, made up of dark Oklahoma dirt. We were in the middle of a dust storm. I took my shirt off and tied it around my face to keep from getting that dirt in my lungs. We crawled under a wagon and stayed there until it blew over. It took a full half hour for it to pass by. I thought that dirt was going to pile up and bury me alive."

That story led to another about the strange sites Daddy had seen along Route 66. There were strange and exotic attractions along that important road. Daddy described a huge metal whale that rested in a shallow pond, a building shaped like a milk bottle, and dozens of other sites designed to attract travelers. I sure would have enjoyed seeing some of those things.

"Why is it called the Mother Road?" Momma asked.

"Because, like a mother holds the family together, this road connects the country," he answered. "The poor Okie farmers are using it every day to go to California. Many of them have lost their farms, and there is no work for them. It's either move on, or starve to death."

We listened, our mouths agape as he described his adventures. Clark and Jerry drifted off to sleep but not us. We were hungry for information. Melba sat on one side of me and Wanda on the other. As Daddy talked, Wanda laid her head over on my shoulder and whispered words that she had never said before and would never say again. "I love you, Jean."

We both knew that she was thinking about what that Pritchert boy had said and how I had defended her. "I love you too," I replied, and I really meant it. We were family, and family sticks together through thick and thin.

Chapter Eight

Purple Rose Buttons

Two important things happened that next week. Grandma and Grandpa came back home and I got a job. Mrs. Estes walked over one afternoon and talked to Momma about me going to work for her. She was a widow woman and lived all alone. Her husband had been a pretty successful button salesman. He had died back a year or so ago and left Mrs. Estes pretty well fixed for money but powerfully lonely. Momma let me sit in when she talked to Mrs. Estes, and I listened and learned a heap that day as they worked out a deal.

"The boys are grown and gone, and I find that I get lonesome," Mrs. Estes began. Even though she was small, she had a confidence about her that belayed her size. "Ruby, what I want is to give Jean a paying job. She could come and live with me while y'all are staying here with Ola and Jon. I know that just as soon as Bill is back on his feet, you'll be moving on, but I sure could use her company for a spell."

Momma put her arm around me protectively and gave me a quick squeeze. "You must feel all alone in that big ole house, Ms. Estes, but I can't just give Jean over to you. She's my child."

Mrs. Estes looked over at me and smiled. "I think we'd get along real good, don't you, Jean?" she tried to draw me into the conversation. Actually, I did like Mrs. Estes. The fact that she couldn't stop herself from eating one of the pies before the forth of July impressed me to no end. I just wasn't sure that I wanted to go live with her.

Momma looked at me with a question in her eyes. I didn't know what she wanted me to say, so I just said what I was thinking. "I like you just fine Ms. Estes, but I would miss Melba and my family too much to come and live with you."

Mrs. Estes pondered on that for a second. "Okay, what if you were to come over in the afternoons, say four o'clock or there about, and spend the nights with me? You could come back home in the mornings? I could pay you a quarter a week."

A quarter was big money to me, and I was ready to jump at the chance. Most of the time Mrs. Estes was talking about would be spent sleeping, so it sounded like a good deal. Momma didn't seem quiet as impressed as me. "Jean sure does help out a lot here," she hedged.

Mrs. Estes jumped in with a counter offer. "How about fifty cents a week?"

Momma sat up a little straighter. "She would just have to come over in the afternoon and spend the night?"

Mrs. Estes could see that she was drawing close to closing the deal. "That's it. She could help me out a bit with supper and a few household chores, but I wouldn't have her doing any heavy work. I'm not looking for a servant."

Momma looked down at me. "What do you think?" she asked.

"That sounds good to me," I replied. I tried really hard to sound all businesslike, just like Momma, but inside I was jumping up and down. That fifty cents a week was spent in my head a thousand times before I had my nightclothes together to go home with Mrs. Estes.

Those first few nights were a tad awkward. For all of her money, Mrs. Estes didn't have a radio, so we had to find things to talk about from the time I got there until it was time for bed. I mentioned the problem to Momma, and she told me that Mrs. Estes was probably hungry to talk to anybody about anything since she lived all alone. I took to telling her the stories we had listened to on the radio, and she seemed to like that a lot.

Mrs. Estes let me help her fix supper and wash the dishes, but I figured out pretty quickly the real reason she wanted me at her home. Poor Mrs. Estes was afraid to stay by herself at night. What she thought an eleven-year-old girl could do to protect her if someone broke in was beyond me, but I seemed to put her fears to rest. Maybe she had heard about the number I played on Milton Pritchert and figured I was as good as a bull dog if things came down to a fight.

Grandma and Grandpa lived about a mile from town, but Mrs. Estes lived right on the edge, not far from the railroad tracks. At least a couple of times a week, a hobo from the train would stop by Mrs. Estes' house to beg for food. Some of these men were just down on their luck, but a few of them were kind of scary. I mentioned this to Daddy and asked him whether or not he thought Mrs. Estes should buy a gun. Daddy was pretty smart about these things. When I walked over to her house that afternoon, he went with me. It took a long time for us to get there, because Daddy had to stop from time to time, but he wanted to talk to Mrs. Estes in person.

While I knocked on the front door, Daddy sank into one of the rocking chairs on Mrs. Estes' front porch. He was plumb tuckered out, but that wasn't the reason he didn't go inside. Momma had explained to me a long time ago that it didn't look right if a man went into a woman's house without either her husband or his wife being there. It didn't seem to matter that Mrs. Estes was older than dirt. This was a hard and fast rule.

"Daddy wants to talk to you for a bit," I explained when Mrs. Estes came to the door.

She took one look at the sweat running down his face and took pity on him. "Go get your daddy something to drink, Sweetie," she told me.

When I came back, they were already talking about the hobo situation. "Find out if he's just down on his luck or if he's a good for nothing bum," Daddy said.

"How do I do that?" Mrs. Estes wanted to know.

"Ask him to do some little job like chopping a bit of firewood or hoeing a row in your garden. If he is willing to do that, leave some food and some water out for him. If he doesn't want to do any work, tell him that you don't have any food to spare."

Mrs. Estes looked real interested in what Daddy was saying. She was nodding at his advice. "Mr. Estes had a gun, but I never learned how to use it. Do you think I need to get it out?" she asked.

Daddy stretched to relieve the pain in his back. "Guns can be a little bit tricky. First off, you have to learn to use one, and second they have to be cleaned and maintained. If you want to learn, I'll show you, but you might want to consider getting a dog. A good pet can be just as much of a discouragement, and a dog stays on duty day and night."

Daddy stayed for a few minutes longer. Mrs. Estes asked him all kinds of questions about dogs and guns and how to deal with hobos. It seemed to relieve her mind to talk to a man about her problems.

That night, I finally got up the nerve to ask Mrs. Estes if I could look at something that had stirred my curiosity. She had five jugs full to the brim of buttons, and those buttons intrigued me. "Mrs. Estes, how did you get all of the buttons?" I asked as we finished supper.

"You know Mr. Estes was a button salesman. He traveled all around the state and into southern Missouri and eastern Tennessee selling buttons to stores." She always got a far away look on her face when she talked about Mr. Estes. I guessed that she missed him something terrible. "When the company changed the style of the buttons, he would bring home the old ones for me to use on my clothes. Over the years, I just collected all of them. There was no way I could sew enough clothes to use them all."

"After supper, do you think we could take them down and look at them?" I asked eagerly.

She actually looked happy about the prospect. "I don't see why not," she answered. It seemed to me that she hurried through our meal and did the dishes in record time.

It was almost like discovering a treasure, as we poured the first jug out onto the table. A purple button that was shaped just like a rose caught my attention. It was probably more suited to the dress of an older woman, but I loved that button on sight. When I held it close to the lamp, it shimmered and seemed to reflect different colors. I saw green and gold and traces of pink. Within seconds, I was searching for more buttons of the same kind.

"Just look at this one," I said in wonder.

"Yes, that one is iridescent. That's what it's called when something picks up more than one color," Mrs. Estes explained.

As I picked through the hundreds of round treasures, Mrs. Estes found buttons that brought back precious memories for her. There was a yellow button that was shaped just like a duck. "Oh this brings back the past.

I used this one on a tiny little shirt I made for Bobby when he was just a baby."

I tried to give it the appropriate amount of attention, before digging back into the still undiscovered treasures. "That's real cute." I commented.

"Would you like to take some of these buttons?" Mrs. Estes asked.

"Yes!" I answered, and spent a few minutes telling Mrs. Estes which buttons I had picked out and how they would look on different dresses for Melba, Wanda, and Momma. Mrs. Estes seemed almost as excited as I was as I described the different garments and how the buttons would set them off just right.

The next afternoon when I arrived at Mrs. Estes' house, she had a wonderful surprise for me. My excitement must have motivated her to do something extra special. She had bought a good length of print cloth. Enough, she explained to make dresses for Melba, Wanda, Momma and me. The best thing was that the print looked good with all of the buttons I had picked out.

Mrs. Estes wasn't a touchy, feely kind of woman. I never once saw her hug anyone. But right then, I didn't care about that. I threw myself at her and gave her a big ole bear hug that almost toppled her over. She acted like she didn't know what to do for just a second, then she laughed and hugged me back. After supper we got down some of her patterns and talked about what would look pretty on Momma and us girls.

The only sad part of the night was when I discovered that there weren't enough of those purple rose buttons for my dress. I was just sure there had been more of them the night before, but we could only come up with two. Mrs. Estes was sympathetic, but quickly showed me some other buttons she thought would look even better. Looking back, I wonder if she knew those buttons wouldn't look good on my dress, so perhaps she hid some of those purple beauties. When I got home in the morning, I couldn't wait to tell Momma and the girls about the surprise. That afternoon when I walked back over to Mrs. Estes' home, Momma and my sisters went with me. Mrs. Estes had a whole cabinet full of Butterick dress patterns and she let us examine each and every one of them. As a button salesman, Mr. Estes had made a lot of connections in the sewing business.

"Goodness gracious, Mrs. Estes," Momma said. "You are better outfitted than some of the dressmaking shops."

Mrs. Estes seemed excited about making our dresses. "I've always envied Ola for having all of you girls. It's so much more fun to sew for girls than it is for boys."

Long after my family went back to Grandma and Grandpa's, Mrs. Estes and I laid out patterns and cut out the fabric.

"Tomorrow," she said, "I'll get started sewing them."

"Do you think you could wait until I get here? I could come early."

She fingers ran up and down the fabric. "I was just about your age when my momma showed me how to sew. We'll get started just as soon as you get here."

By the time the pieces were cut out, there were hundreds of scraps and threads on the floor. I gladly swept and tidied up before bedtime. That night I went to bed wondering how I could find more of those beautiful purple buttons.

Mrs. Estes had more patience than anyone I had ever met. I was fascinated by her Singer treadle sewing machine. Momma was a talented woman, but she had never learned the art of garment making. My employer showed me how to make sure the arrows lined up and the pattern piece was straight with the nap of the fabric. She explained that if we cut it crooked, the dress wouldn't hang right. Mrs. Estes showed me how to mark for darts. She let me thread a needle with brightly colored thread and showed me how to stick the needle through the fabric and pattern at the large dot on the pattern that marked the end of the dart. "Leave a long, long tail on that thread," she warned. "If you don't it will pull through when you have to separate the fabric. If that happens, we'll have to put the pattern back on to mark the darts."

Even though I was older than Melba, we were about the same size. I learned how to fold the pattern down and pin it into place, for our shorter waistlines. Every afternoon for three days, I raced to Mrs. Estes' house to work on those dresses. On the straight stretches of the seams, Mrs. Estes let me do part of the stitching on the machine, but when it came to the collars and sleeves, she did all of the work. The treadle sewing machine didn't need electricity to work. In order to make the machine go, the seamstress worked a paddle, located at the bottom of the machine. Mrs. Estes was masterful at this. Her foot seemed to fly back and forth on that foot paddle and the fabric zipped by under the moving needle.

When all the machine work was done, Mrs. Estes and I started on the handwork. Before turning me loose on the actual dresses, she made me practice hemming and sewing on buttons on an old scrap of material. When I got good enough, she taught me how to turn up the hemline and measure the sem. "You have to turn it up exactly the same all the way around the whole dress," she explained. "If you don't, your dress will be longer on one side than the other. You'd have to walk crooked to make it look straight." She made me laugh when she did a lopsided walk to demonstrate.

That last day of work on the dresses, Momma came over with me. She offered to crochet scalloped lace for the collars, if Mrs. Estes thought that would that would look good. They agreed that the lace would set off the dresses beautifully. Momma's fingers were as fast with a crochet needle as Mrs. Estes' foot had been with the machine paddle. She did all four collars and still made it home before dark. Mrs. Estes ooohhhed and aaaahhed over Momma's fine work. Before she left, Momma thanked

Mrs. Estes for the dresses and her kind treatment of me. She also offered to make lace for any of Mrs. Estes' dresses. When we were alone, I tried on my dress one more time. As much as I liked it, I got the feeling that it made Mrs. Estes happier than it did me. She really did miss having a daughter. In my opinion, that was just a crying shame, especially since she had all of those buttons and patterns just going to waste. Little did we know that I would soon be wearing my new dress to a funeral.

Chapter Nine

The Waving Ferryman

The weather was hotter than ever as we trudged through August. Temperatures soared over 110 degrees on a daily basis. Late one afternoon, a fast moving car pulled up to the house and came to a screeching halt. A rather large woman jumped out and started yelling for Grandma. The woman was puffing by the time she reached the porch. I didn't know whether it was fear, which was so clearly written on her face, or the fact that she was so large, but she was heaving for every breath.

"Ms. Ola," she said, but it barely came out. Clark started yelling for Grandma and she came running real quickly.

The woman had sunk down onto the porch steps and tried to catch her breath. I ran for a dipper full of water and handed it to her just about the time Grandma rounded the house.

It was obvious that Grandma knew this woman. "Mary," Grandma said as she rushed up. "What's wrong?"

"It's Bill. He's collapsed. Out in the car," she gasped out in short, choppy gulps as she motioned with her hand.

Now this caused some confusion. Daddy's name was Bill. He had left out that morning with Grandpa. If he had collapsed, where was Grandpa? Surely, he wouldn't just send Daddy home with this strange woman.

As I rushed out to check on Daddy, I discovered a different Bill altogether. Stretched out in the back seat of the car, this Bill was a lot bigger and his face was red as a ripe tomato. Grandma moved me to the side as she opened the back door to examine the patient. Her hands moved over his red face, and she yelled over to the woman on the porch. "Mary, he's burning up hot. Has he been sick?"

Mary just shook her head and yelled back. "No. He was out on the ferryboat all day and I think the heat must have gotten to him. One of the men brought him home a few minutes ago. He said Bill just fell down, and they couldn't wake him up."

Grandma looked at me. "We're going to have to get him in some cold water fast. Run down to the garden and get your Momma and Aunt. Tell the boys to get the tub down and have Melba and Wanda draw plenty of water from the well."

I ran to follow Grandma's instructions. There were no men to help, so grandma ended up dragging the man out of the car and laying him on a blanket. From there, we all pulled and tugged until we got him around the house to the back porch. On the backside of the house, the porch was lower so it didn't take as much effort to get him up onto it as it would have on the front side of the house. The tub was about half way full by the time we lowered him into the water. I would like to say that we gently placed him in the tub, but that wasn't the way it happened. We were tugging with all of our might and had Bill lifted above the tub when one side of the blanket slipped and he plopped into the water like a limp fish. Water sloshed out and Grandma supported his head to make sure that it didn't dip below the water.

That man was so hot that the cool bath heated up and was quite warm within a few minutes. Grandma sent us girls to chip off some ice to cool it down. When we got back, Grandma was explaining to Mary what was happening to her husband.

"He's got the heat stroke. His temperature is sky high," Grandma gently said.

"But he'll be okay, right?" Mary wanted some reassurance.

I could tell from the look on Grandma's face that she didn't really think so. It was like she was wrestling with herself, deciding how much to tell Mary. "He could be, but most of the time heat stroke this bad doesn't turn out good."

"But he'll live?"

What Grandma tried to explain to Mary was that sometimes living isn't the best thing, but Mary wasn't ready to hear that.

"He could, but if he does, he probably won't be the same ever again," Grandma said.

Mary heard what she wanted to hear. She grasped onto the prospect that her husband had a chance to live and that he might be okay, but she didn't listen to anything else. Grandma called a doctor over in Jonesboro and talked to him for a long while. When she got off the telephone, she didn't look any more confident.

I walked to work right on schedule at four o'clock. Mrs. Estes had grown up with Bill and insisted that we go back to my grandparents to see if there was anything we could do to help out. All the rest of that day and well into the night, Grandma tended to Bill. As word spread, friends and neighbors came from all around. The preacher showed up and talked to Grandma before leading us all in a prayer.

"Dear Lord," he said in a soft voice, "we come to you today on behalf of our good friend Bill Dentrick. Dear God, you know what is on our hearts. We want our brother brought back to us in good health, Lord. Please dear God, guide the hands of Ms. Ola as she treats our dear friend. And Lord, if it is Bill's time to go on to you, Lord please accept him into your welcome arms."

Grandma and Grandpa's already crowded house was close to bursting open. Some of the crowd almost took on a party mood, laughing and telling jokes, while their friend lay near to death on my grandparents' bed. Things began to quiet down around eleven o'clock. Some people went home; others made pallets for their kids and continued to sit vigil. A little after one o'clock in the morning, Mr. Dentrick passed away.

Mary wailed and cried as the preacher offered comfort and her friends stood nearby, weeping quietly and wondering what they could do to help her through this terrible tragedy. After a time, some of the men offered to take Bill's body home. The preacher helped them work out a schedule of people who were willing to sit with the body until the funeral.

It wasn't until the next day that I realized that Mr. Bill Dentrick was the nice man who waved us on to the ferryboat when we crossed the river. That made me extra sad. It didn't seem so bad when he was just some stranger. For the first time, I realized that every time somebody dies, it's not just a story in the newspaper or on the radio. Some family is hurting a powerful lot.

Even though we were plumb tuckered out, Momma made us get up at our regular time the next morning. She said that this was a lesson we had to learn. Sometimes bad things happen, but you have to keep going. Momma and Aunt Lorene spent the morning cooking.

Momma wiped sweat off her face with the sleeve of her dress. "The Dentricks have a big family, so they'll need plenty to eat."

Aunt Lorene glanced up from the batter she was mixing for a plain white cake. "They'll have more than they can ever use, but if there's a problem, throwing more food at it can't hurt." She and Momma chuckled together. It did seem that almost any problem could be solved with a covered dish.

The whole family went to take the food and visit the Dentrick's. Mary was kind of in a daze. She talked to Momma and Aunt Lorene, but wouldn't say a word to Grandma. On the way home, Grandma explained when things don't turn out so well, the family sometimes blames the person who has tried to help them. I knew that Mrs. Dentrick was hurting, but this made me kind of mad at her. My Grandma took care of half the county and she never asked anyone for anything in return. How dare Mrs. Dentrick treat her like this?

When we got home, I sat out on the front porch with Grandpa. I mentioned to him how angry I was, and he sympathized with me.

Grandpa got a far-off look on his face and talked about Grandma's profession. "I remember back in '18 when the flu epidemic struck. Your grandma had her own horse and buggy. She was gone for two straight weeks tending to folks who were struck down with the flu. Never once did she think about her own health. She did worry about bringing it home to the kids and me, but she couldn't keep from helping those people who were afflicted and needed her."

I was mighty confused. "Why do they blame her when all she does is try to help them?"

Grandpa was a wise man. He explained it like this. "These are God-loving people, Jean. They know that they can't put the blame off on God. So, they look for some other place for it. Sometimes, it lands on your grandma. The truth of the matter is we were never meant to live on this earth forever. There's a time when we need to move on to the next life, but the people who are left behind just aren't ready to let go."

Mr. Bill Dentrick's funeral was the next day, and the church building was packed full of mourners. It was miserably hot and everybody searched the back of the pews for loose paper or cardboard to use as a fan. Before the family was brought in, Momma sent us kids outside. She told us to find a shade tree and wait until the service was over. It was such a relief to be outside that we explored the graveyard, looking at all of the headstones. The ones for the babies just about broke my heart. Melba and I almost worked ourselves up to a cry, but Wanda brought us back to earth. "If they were babies, they are now in the hands of Jesus," she explained. "That has got to be better than living here in this heat."

Clark and Jerry wandered over close to the open grave where Mr. Dentrick's body would soon be laid to rest. Melba and I had to go drag them away to keep one or both of them from falling in.

"I don't want to go, and you can't make me," Jerry argued.

Melba put her hands on her hips just like we had seen Momma do. "Yes, you do. Aunt Lorene told you to mind us."

"Nu huh," Clark argued.

"I say we let them be," Wanda interjected with her precise speech. We all looked at her like she was crazy. "If they fall in, they will just lower that casket down on top of them and we'll have more room at Grandma's house."

Clark and Jerry couldn't get away from that hole fast enough. They came out untouched, but their clothing didn't. While the boys had red clay mud all over their nice clothes, our new dresses came out unscathed. Aunt Lorene griped about their sorry state all the way home. Before long, those muddy clothes were forgotten. Without even trying, Jerry found a way to impress the whole family.

Chapter Ten
Old Man Huff Comes a Begging

We heard on the radio that Jesse Owens had won four Olympic gold medals in Germany. This was the most gold medals any American had ever won. According to the announcer, a man named Adolf Hitler didn't like that much on account of the fact that Mr. Owens was a negro. Daddy said the color of a man's skin didn't matter much. It was how fast he ran that counted in the Olympic Games. I wondered why they called them games. All of that running seemed like a lot of hard work to me.

Before we knew it, we could tell that the days were getting shorter and we were seeing the first days of September. Even though the state didn't have the money to pay all of the teachers, school started. Momma and Aunt Lorene took us down the first day and enrolled us in class. At the age of six, Clark began his first year in school, but Jerry wasn't old enough. Every afternoon he sat out on the front porch and waited for us to get home. Melba and I made friends easily enough, but Wanda just didn't know how to fit in. Even though she was older, she ended up hanging out with us. She could be annoying, but we couldn't tell her to leave us alone. Momma once told us that you can pick your friends, but you are stuck with family. We promised to look out for one another, and held that promise like it was a sacred oath.

Most of the garden plants were finally dying down. After the late potatoes were dug, Grandpa hitched up his mules and turned the garden soil. We planted turnips and mustards greens and finished harvesting apples from the orchard. Things weren't as busy as they had been in the summer, but we found plenty to keep us busy.

We didn't wear our new dresses every Sunday, but every other one for sure. The second Tuesday of the month, Mrs. Estes got a letter from her son, Bobby. He wanted her to come for a visit. Bobby had even included a train ticket to St. Louis. When I got to her house that afternoon, she was wringing her boney hands with worry. Since opening the letter, she had done nothing but fret about the reason for the invitation. "Do you think he's sick?" she asked me. "Or, maybe he's lost his job. People are out of work all over the place."

"Now think about that, Mrs. Estes," I tried to reassure her. "If he had lost his job, do you think he would spend money on a train ticket? Maybe they have good news, or don't you think that he just misses you? If I lived that far from my momma, I sure would miss her."

Mrs. Estes stopped pacing and sat down beside me. "That's the reason I like you so much, Jean. You are such a sensible young lady."

That night I helped Mrs. Estes pack for her trip. Her train didn't leave until Saturday noon, and she didn't know how long she would be gone. She dragged out a bunch of dresses and three pairs of shoes and put them into the fancy travel bag she would use to carry her stuff. Once again, I was the voice of reason. "Doesn't your son have a wash tub for you to wash your clothes?" I asked. "It's sure going to be heavy for you carry all of this by yourself." I didn't want to point out that she was an old lady, but she must have gotten the point.

She finally decided on four dresses, one of them kind of fancy, and two pairs of shoes. As I drifted off to sleep that night, I realized that I was losing my job, at least for a little while. Grandpa took Mrs. Estes to the train station and he let me ride along.

I missed her more than I thought I would, but it felt good to be back home full time. Although fall was not far away, the days were still hot. Grandpa was busier than ever. The farmers used the summer to give their cows a chance to fatten up before getting them ready to sell in the fall. Most days, Grandpa left right after breakfast. He spent his days going from farm to farm, examining the cows and offering advice to help the farmers get the best price for their herds.

On Wednesday morning, right before we left for school, a man showed up at the house. He didn't look a lot older than Daddy, but he was unkempt in appearance. I listened as Grandma talked to him and then led him to the lot where Grandpa kept his mules, Sassy and Bolt.

"I don't mind you taking the mules to turn your garden Mr. Huff, but we would appreciate it if you would treat them well. Those mules are almost like family, so I'll leave it to you to keep 'em well watered and fed."

Mr. Huff talked a good talk. He "yepped" and "uh huhed" and made big promises. "Ms. Ola, I'll treat them mules just like they were mine."

Grandma was a smart cookie. She didn't leave it at that. "No sir, Mr. Huff. I'd appreciate it if you would treat them like they were mine."

Mr. Huff took Sassy and Bolt and we saw neither hide nor hair of him until way past dark. He brought the mules back lathered with sweat and hungry to boot. He didn't even come up to the house to let Grandma know they were back. He just turned them out in the lot and went on his way.

That night at supper, Grandpa was fit to be tied. "I drove past the Garner place this afternoon and couldn't believe my eyes. There was old man Huff, using our mules to turn their garden. From what I hear, he used our mules to make some extra money for himself and didn't even have the decency to feed them."

By this time, the whole family was mad at that old Mr. Huff. Poor Sassy and Bolt. "I'll tell you one thing,"

Grandpa said as he pointed his fork to no one in particular. "Old man Huff neen to ever ask to borrow my mules again."

In the South, people sometimes take two or more words and squeeze them together to make a whole new word. "Neen" was one of those words, and it meant "need not." So Grandpa was saying that no way, no how was Mr. Huff ever in a million years going to have use of Sassy and Bolt again. My sweet tempered grandpa ranted and raved about Mr. Huff until bedtime.

Just a few minutes after Grandpa left the next morning, we saw Mr. Huff walking toward the house. Clark, my sisters, and I were just leaving for school when he made his way up to the house. Little Jerry was sitting on the top step, just like he did every morning when we left him for the day.

"Mr. Huff," Jerry said when the man got within hearing distance.

Mr. Huff ignored Jerry and kept walking.

Little Jerry spoke up a little louder. "Mr. Huff!"

Finally Mr. Huff slowed down a little. "Yes son?" he said, but he didn't stop walking toward the door.

"My Granddaddy said you neen to eeeevvvver ask to borrow his mules again," Jerry said.

Jerry now had a little bit of Mr. Huff's attention. He paused. "What's that you say, son?"

This time Jerry belted it out. Mr. Huff would have had to be stone deaf to keep from hearing him. "My Granddaddy said you neen to eeeeevvvver ask to borrow his mules again. He said that aaannnybody who would use a man's mules for gain and not even feed or water them was just good for nothing."

Mr. Huff's hand was raised to knock on the door, but it suddenly dropped to his side. He didn't say another word. He just turned around and walked back the way he came. Up to this point, Jerry had been nothing but a little nuisance. But suddenly, he was pretty big and important in our eyes. Aunt Lorene and Momma came out onto the porch and took Jerry back inside with them. They were both laughing like crazy.

When we got home from school, Melba, Wanda and I got some of the wormy apples and fed the mules a little extra treat. They deserved a little pampering. We didn't know it at the time, but those poor mules weren't the only ones in the family who would be eating bugs and such.

Chapter Eleven

Rice Pudding . . . Yum

Mrs. Russell stood at the front of the class with the list of spelling words. School wasn't so bad. I had a new best friend, next to Melba, of course. Her name was Ina Lee Jackson and we hit it off just fine. Melba was just as sweet as ever and had a passel of friends. As amazing as it seemed to all of us, Wanda even had a boyfriend. He seemed to love her bossy attitude. Grandpa said that some men just like a woman who will tell them what to do. If that was the case, Willy McCloud was in hog heaven. Wanda bossed that boy ever which way to Sunday. The McCloud's owned the only grocery store in Newark and they were one of the few families in the area who had a telephone. Suddenly my grandparents' telephone was ringing every night, one long and two shorts. Wanda chatted a few minutes every day with her boyfriend. Ever once in a while, Daddy would complain that no one else would be able to get through if there was an emergency. Like always, Wanda just ignored him and went on talking to Willy. My mind wandered to these things instead of the spelling test I was about to take.

"Government," Mrs. Russell said, and then used it in a sentence. "The president is a part of the *government*."

Jackie Werner was the class clown. He piped up from the back of the room. "Or, the government is flat broke." Every student laughed and then turned back to the test paper.

"G-O-V-E-R-N-M-E-N-T," I wrote.

Mrs. Russell strolled up and down the rows between the desks. "The next word is *either*," she said, using the long "e" pronunciation. "Or either," she continued, using the long "i" pronunciation. "I will choose *either* the blue dress or the red dress."

Freda Melton raised her hand and waited for Mrs. Russell to notice her. "Yes Freda?"

"If it's okay with you, Mrs. Russell, I'm going to spell it *either*," Freda said, pronouncing it with the long "i."

Mrs. Russell's lips turned up in a small smile. She didn't embarrass Freda by telling her that the word could be pronounced either way but the spelling was the same. "That's fine, Freda," she said.

When I turned in my paper, I had every confidence that I had aced the test. Spelling was one of my best subjects, as was math. I almost never had to study for a test, except in history. I liked to learn the stories, but hated to memorize the dates.

About midday, Clark's teacher came into my classroom. She quietly spoke to Mrs. Russell and then motioned for me to the front of the class.

"Clark threw up right after lunch. I thought maybe he just played too hard, but now he is complaining about his stomach hurting. Maybe it would be best if you took him home," Mrs. Wallis explained.

"Yes ma'am," I responded and followed Clark's teacher out of the room.

I couldn't help but feel sorry for the little boy. On the way home, we had to stop twice more for him to puke in the bushes. Momma always felt of my head to see if I was running a fever when I was sick, so I tried to do the same for Clark. His head might have felt a little warm, but I couldn't really tell whether or not he was feverish. By the time we got home, he was as white as a sheet and clutching his stomach. I turned him over to Aunt Lorene and ran all the way back to school. By the time I rushed into my classroom, school was ending for the day. I had just enough time to get my homework assignments for the day before Wanda and Melba and I walked back home.

Poor Clark was sick all that night. I heard Aunt Lorene get up with him off and on several times. He wasn't throwing up anymore, but he did have diarrhea. After a few trips to the outhouse, Aunt Lorene got a night pot and put it close to his bed. We all stayed as far away from him as we could, which was hard since we were all stuck in the same small house together. His sickness lasted clear through the week. By the weekend, he was finally feeling better, and miracle of miracles none of the rest of us got sick.

Aunt Lorene was still feeding Clark bland foods, but he was clamoring for some food that tasted good. About noontime, Mrs. Eunice Williams came calling. According to Grandma, she was the best neighbor in the whole world, but she was tighter than the bark on a tree. She never threw anything away, no matter its condition. That day, she came bearing a gift.

Ms. Eunice place a covered dish on the kitchen table and bent down to speak to my cousin. "Clark, honey," she said. "I heard about the spell you've been having with your stomach. Is it all better?"

"Yes ma'am," he answered. "My belly's feeling lots better, but Momma still won't let me eat much. She says maybe by tomorrow."

"A little birdie told me that rice pudding is your favorite dessert. Is that right?"

It had been days and days since Clark had tasted anything but thin broth and water. Just the mention of something as rich and delicious as rice pudding set his taste buds to watering. "Yes ma'am! It sure is. I just plumb love rice pudding."

"Well I made a whole dish of it just for you. You don't even have to share a bite of it with Jerry or the girls," Ms. Eunice informed the boy.

"Yippee," Clark exclaimed. Before anyone could stop him, he raced to the kitchen for a spoon. He dug right into that rice pudding without even putting it out onto a plate. He just ate right from the dish. As Clark ate one bite after another, Ms. Eunice told us about preparing her special dish.

"I got the rice from Ollie Whitlow. Do you know him Ola?" Ms. Eunice asked Grandma.

"Of course, I doctored his wife last winter when she came down with pneumonia," Grandma answered. "It was touch and go for a few days."

"Well, this year when I was canning my potatoes, I gave him a bunch of peelings for his hogs."

The conversation was kind of getting boring, so Melba and I pulled out our homework and went to work on it. I listened to the adult conversation with one ear and reviewed my history lesson with the other. History just about put me to sleep, so listening to the adults was actually a good thing. Besides, I was known in the family as the one who liked to eves drop. Truth be told, I could be a bit nosy.

"So," Ms. Eunice continued. "Ollie dropped off this rice. He said it was for my chickens on account of the fact that it was full of bugs."

Poor Clark stopped eating mid bite and looked up from his favorite dish. My homework was forgotten. We were all suddenly hanging onto every word coming from Ms. Eunice's mouth. "I put that dried rice into a deep bowl, added some water, and those bugs just floated to the top. Once I scraped them off, that rice was as good as any."

Clark made it to the back door before throwing up every bite he had just eaten. Aunt Lorene ran after Clark. Momma cleared her throat, and Grandma did what Grandma did best. She smoothed things over. "Maybe Clark wasn't quite ready to start eating again. You know how these things are. You feel better one minute, and you're sick again the next."

Ms. Eunice stayed and visited a few minutes before heading home. We could hear Clark crying and Aunt Lorene trying to sooth him in a hushed voice. The instant Ms. Eunice was out of sight, Grandma let out a deep breath. "Don't, under any circumstances, eat anything that woman cooks," she told us. "We went to her house for dinner one night, and she served us fish head soup!"

We wanted to laugh, but we all felt so sorry for poor little Clark that we bit our tongues and held it back. Bless his heart, he had been through enough. For the next twenty-four hours, he didn't complain about water and thin broth. By Monday, he was still a little weak but able to go to school.

Mrs. Russell decided to give us a pop quiz during history class. About half way through, I was wishing that I had spent more time studying and less time listening to the buggy-rice story.

When I got to the fifth question, I was stuck. "The French Indian war ended in what year?"

In my mind's eye, I could clearly picture that section of the chapter in my book. There was a drawing of a wild looking man on the page. My book was right below my chair. Mrs. Russell was sitting at her desk with her head down. It wouldn't take me but just a second to find that page in the book. For as long as I could remember, my eyes had been weak. In order for me to see the page, I had to hold the book right up close to my nose. Just as I got to the right place, Mrs. Russell spoke from the front of the classroom.

"Jean, put your book away," she said.

My face turned bright red. Even my ears flamed hot. I quickly put my book away and went back to my test. Mrs. Russell could have made it a lot worse on me. When it was time to go out for recess, she called me to her desk.

"Jean, I'm not going to punish you for looking at your book this time," she gently told me. "But I want you to understand why it's wrong to cheat."

There it was on the table. She had said the word. Cheat. A lot of kids did it, but nobody wanted to be known as one. Because I had been blessed with a good mind, I had never been tempted to cheat before.

"Yes maam," I mumbled, unable to meet her eyes.

She gently reached over, hooked her finger under my chin and raised my face until I was looking at her straight. "Cheating doesn't hurt anybody but you. If you don't learn this stuff, you'll never get a good education."

"But why do I have to know about the French Indian War? How is that ever going to help me in life?" I asked.

Mrs. Russell sat back in her chair. "Some of this must seem like a lot of foolishness to you. To be truthful, I don't always understand why we need to learn everything that we do. But I know this. History is important because it teaches us about the mistakes people have made in the past and that helps us to avoid those same mistakes in the future. Just think, what if the officials in our government had studied history. Would we be in this depression?"

"But why is that important to me?" I wanted to know.

"Because, you never know what you are going to do when you grow up. What if you want to be a teacher, like me? You'll never pass the teacher exam unless you get it now. You're a smart girl, but nobody is so smart that they can't learn something new. What if you grow up to be a politician?"

"I'm a girl," I argued. "I can't run for office."

"Now, little lady, if you knew your *history*, you would know that Mrs. Hattie Caraway is a United States Senator, and she is from right here in Arkansas."

Up until that moment, I never thought about what I wanted to do when I grew up. I just assumed that I would be a wife and mother, like Momma. Those things took a different kind of education. I was learning skills from Momma every day. But what if I wanted to become a teacher? Or what if I married and my husband left me like Uncle Jim had left Aunt Lorene. What if I wanted to do something different all together? Shoot fire, maybe I did want to become a Senator from the great state of Arkansas.

I stared Mrs. Russell right in the eye. "I understand. When I cheat, I only cheat myself. I promise I won't ever do it again." And I didn't either, not once.

Chapter Twelve
It's a Sign

Mrs. Estes road the train back into Newark, and Grandpa and I met her at the depot. She had called ahead to let us know when she would be arriving. I saw her just as soon as she got off the train. Grandpa found her bag and loaded it into the back of the truck. It was obvious that she was bursting with news. I had never seen her so excited.

"You were right, Jean. All that time, I worried for nothing," she said as she grabbed me in a hug. "I'm going to be a grandmother. That's what Bobby wanted to tell me."

This was the grandest news I could imagine. A baby was just what Mrs. Estes needed. Her life was too sad and lonely. A baby would change all of that. Grown men got all mushy around a sweet little baby.

"That's wonderful, Mrs. Estes!" I said when she finally released me. "I just knew it was something good."

I climbed up into Grandpa's truck, and Mrs. Estes followed me. Grandpa shut the door for us and walked around to his side of the truck. After he got behind the wheel and started the truck, he turned to Mrs. Estes. "That's real good news, Phoebe." Up to that point, I didn't know Mrs. Estes' first name. Phoebe suited her just right. "I remember when Ruby was expecting Jean. We couldn't wait for her to get here. Are you going to go back to St. Louis when the time comes?"

"Nope," Mrs. Estes said with a smile. "I'm not waiting until then. Bobby and Marlene want me to come now. They've asked me to move up there permanently. I think I can have everything squared away by Thanksgiving."

Suddenly, this didn't seem like such good news. My job was moving to the big city and my dreams about all that money I was going to make were drying up on the vine. I wilted down into the seat.

Mrs. Estes seemed to read my mind. "Jean, would you like to help me get my house all squared away for the move. It's likely to take me a month of Sundays. Of course, I'll pay you for your hard work."

Just like a wilted flower put in a glass of water, I perked right up. "That sounds like a fine idea," I replied. "But, I sure am going to miss you, Mrs. Estes."

"Jon, if you would drop by your house, we can see if Melba would like to come and help too. I'd like to get started as soon as possible."

And suddenly, I was back on the payroll and so was my sister. We brought our night gowns and dresses for church the next morning. That night, we stayed up way past our bedtime helping Mrs. Estes go through boxes of junk and treasures. Both of us had a mounding pile of things Mrs. Estes had given us to take home - everything from Butterick dress patterns to the green dishes Mrs. Estes had collected from buying oats. Every time we bought a tin of oats, we couldn't wait to see what dishware was hidden inside, but Momma didn't have half as many of those pretty dishes as Mrs. Estes.

The next morning during worship services, Melba and I leaned on each other and slept through most of the sermon. When the congregation stood up to sing, I just about jumped out of my skin. Melba slept right through that song and the three others that followed. That afternoon, we went back to work for Mrs. Estes. Grandpa had promised to come and get us at dark. By the time he got there, we had boxes of goodies to take home with us. He helped us load our booty and toted them home without one complaint. It wasn't until we were almost there that we thought about the challenge of fitting all of that extra stuff into Grandma and Grandpa's already crowded house.

"Goodness gracious girls," Grandma threw her hands into the air. "Where in the world do you think we're going to put all of this? Some of it will have to go."

"But Grandma," Melba wailed. "It's all really good stuff. We can't just throw it out."

"Jean," she turned to me. Since I was older, I guess she thought it would be easier to reason with me. Plus, I might have been Grandpa's favorite, but Melba was clearly Grandma's and she didn't want to disappoint her. "We can't keep all of this. We'd have to get rid of one of you kids to make room for it all."

If I got a vote in the matter, I was going to pick Fenetta, but even at eleven, I was too smart to say that. "But Grandma," I argued, "kids are starving in this country. We can't just throw good stuff away."

Grandma was foiled. That was one of her arguments when she thought we were being wasteful. If we heard it once, we heard it a thousand times that summer. "Kids, we can't afford to be wasteful. First of all, God doesn't want us to be wasteful of His blessings, and second, there are kids all over this country who are starving. When you are careless, it's like you are taking food right out of their mouths."

Shoot, we even dried the peals off the apples and peaches for fried pies. When I accidentally dropped one onto the ground, I felt guilty for a good long minute. If I walked around with my conscience paining me most of the summer, it surely wouldn't hurt Grandma to feel guilty for a few minutes. "Maybe we can go through it and get it more organized," Grandma finally consented.

Momma and Aunt Lorene quickly agreed. Personally, I think they were just anxious to rummage through our treasures. When all was said and done, we didn't have to give up one thing. Mrs. Estes believed in buying quality stuff. More than once, Melba and I had to remind the adults that the goodies belonged to us.

As we lay on our pallet that night, we talked about what items we wanted to save for our hope chests. By the time a girl was my age, she had started saving special things that would help her set up housekeeping when she got married. While I didn't have an actual wooden cedar chest yet, I had already started saving. Momma taught me to embroidery, and I had stitched a pretty scene on a set of pillowcases. I also had a rose painted tea set, but two of the cups were chipped, and the lid to the teapot was missing. Slowly, I would add other things to prepare me for that special day.

September slipped away before we knew it, and we drifted into October. Halloween approached, but most families couldn't afford any candy treats, so we just made paper masks out of the pages of an old Sears catalog and decorated them with whatever odds and ends we could find. Willy McCloud brought Wanda some candy from his family's store. We begged and begged for just a bite, but she refused to share any of it with us. Totally confident that none of us would dare steal it, she left it right out on the dresser in Fenetta's bedroom. As bad as I wanted just a lick of one of her suckers, I was too afraid to do something so bold.

The days seemed to creep by, but before we knew it, November was almost over. The temperature was still warmer than normal. The adults talked about the strange fall we were having. Eventually, the weather, just like everything else finally changed. The week before Thanksgiving, the weather finally gave away and we woke up one morning to the cold and wet we had been expecting for some time. It was like the skies opened up and didn't stop pouring for three days straight. Momma had to dig through the boxes we still had packed to get out our winter clothes.

As we could see the holiday's approach, kids at school became restless. The rain didn't help any. The soggy weather kept us from going outside at recess. We played *I Spy* and *How Many Words Can You Make* so many times that I knew every yellow item in the classroom and exactly how many words you could make out of "Thanksgiving is Coming." Friday was a particularly bad day. Grandpa came to get us in the truck. He didn't want us walking home in the thunder and lightening. He dropped me off at Mrs. Estes' house and promised to pick me us up for church on Sunday if the weather stayed bad. Melba no longer came with me to work. Mrs. Estes was just days away from leaving, and most of the work was done.

We worked for a while on Friday night. By Saturday afternoon, Mrs. Estes was just about finished packing up all of her stuff. I could tell that she was anxious to move close to her son but sad at the same time. She had a ticket to catch Monday's Train to St. Louis. That meant we had little time to finish up.

"Did you know that I was born in the house that sat on this very spot?" she said as she lingered over dinner. I was anxious to go through the rest of her stuff, but she needed to talk.

"You were born in this house?" I asked.

"No, not this one. Mamma and Papa's house was torn down years ago when Mr. Estes built this one, but this is the same place. The jonquils that line my walkway were planted by my mamma. I don't guess I'll be seeing them bloom this spring," she sighed.

"Why don't you take some of the jonquil blubs with you?" I suggested. "If I was your son's wife, I sure would like to have flowers that have been in the family for years blooming in my yard. That is something you can share with your new grandbaby."

Suddenly, Mrs. Estes was in motion. She jumped up from the table and clasped her hands together. "Jean, you are a genius," she said. "Why didn't I think of that? And it's a good time of the year to dig the bulbs."

Now, I wouldn't have gone so far as to say that I was a genius, but maybe I was one smart cookie. "Do you want to dig them tonight?" I asked.

She started to clear the table as she spoke. "Not tonight. It's too dark, but I'll do it when I get home from church tomorrow. What a jewel you are. I sure would like to keep in touch with you even after I move. Do you think you could be bothered to write this old lady?"

Mrs. Estes must have been pushing fifty. She probably wasn't going to last much longer. I would kind of enjoy writing back and forth to her for the next couple years or so until she expired of old age. "I'd love to!" I said. "I'll write and tell you what happens to us when Daddy gets another job and we move."

"Say, I've got a great idea," Mrs. Estes said as she walked to the high shelf that held her button jars. "What if I gave you a couple of the jars of my buttons? Every time you make a new garment, you write to me and tell me all about it."

I was too excited to speak. Maybe my gratitude was evident by the way I couldn't quit jumping up and down. "Now you, my little jackrabbit, had better settle down before you work yourself into a tizzy," Mrs. Estes laughed.

As she washed the dishes and I dried them and put them away, Mrs. Estes told me something that was guaranteed to make me skip a tizzy and hop right on to a genuine frenzy. This surprise was enough to keep me wide-awake most of the night.

It might not have been her original plan, but by the time the kitchen was clean and all but one coal oil lamp was turned down and blown out, Mrs. Estes had decided to leave all of her sewing supplies with me. I couldn't believe my ears when she told me that in addition to the patterns, buttons, threads and needles, she was giving me her treadle sewing machine.

"When I think about it, there isn't going to be near enough room for the machine at Bobby's house, especially with the baby coming. It would just get stacked in some storage shed and go to rust. If I give it to you, you have to promise to take care of it."

At that point, I would have probably promised her just about anything she asked. "I will, I will, I will!"

Right before she went to her bedroom and I went to mine, Mrs. Estes got a sweet smile on her face and gave me one more thing to think about. "Now when you sew the perfect dress to use those purple buttons, I'll expect a letter for sure."

Those purple buttons! How I loved them. Gosh, this was kind of like being a rich heiress or something, except that Mrs. Estes hadn't died, which just made it doubly nice. Wanda and Melba would be green with envy, but I would make it up to them by sewing their clothes. The whole family was going to be past excited. I would have to learn to sew more than straight seams. I would have to conquer sleeves and collars too. I envisioned making beautiful silk dresses fit for royalty. As I fell asleep that night, one nagging thought crossed my mind. What was Grandma going to say about me bringing something this big home? Where in the world would we put it?

Chapter 13

Cracklins

"Moooommmmma," Fenetta whined to Grandma. "Why does that horrible piece of furniture have to stay in my room?"

Of course, I had to brag about my gift from Mrs. Estes the second we got to church. Momma looked excited, but she was the only one. I was pretty sure that Fenetta was just jealous. Any argument was cut short when the song leader chose that moment to start the worship service. As we sang **In the Sweet By and By**, Fenetta glared daggers at me, which I returned with a possum-eating grin.

By the time we got home, Grandma's nerves were stretched to their limit. The sermon had been extra long, and two people had responded to the Lord's invitation at the end of the service. Because of the rain, Grandpa drove his truck to church. All of us were stacked in the cab like cord wood. Clark stood on the seat between Grandpa and Grandma. Melba and Wanda sat on Grandma's lap.

Momma and I sat on Aunt Lorene's lap, and little Jerry stretched across the top of all of us. Daddy never went to church with us, which was kind of good, because I don't think there was one inch of space left in that truck. Grandma was completely quiet all the way home. Even Fenetta left her alone.

According to Melba, poor Grandma had been busy all Saturday taking care of a little boy with pneumonia. The Roberts family lived way out in the country and Grandma spent the entire night sitting up with their youngest boy, Richard. Melba had questioned Grandma about the steam tent she had made for him until Grandma was just plumb tuckered out. I realized that she simply didn't have the energy to complain about me dragging home a sewing machine. Nor did she have it in her to respond to Fenetta's protests. As soon as we got home, she went to her bedroom and closed the door. That was the only time I ever remembered Grandma sleeping during the day, but she was all done in.

While Momma and Aunt Lorene fixed Sunday dinner, Grandpa took me over to Mrs. Estes' house to pick up my sewing machine. The sun had finally come out and he thought it would be better to get it while Grandma was sleeping. After we got that beautiful piece of machinery loaded into the truck, I realized what a solemn occasion this was. Mrs. Estes was leaving the next day and this would be the last time I would see her. She cried like a baby when it was time for us to go. I wasn't sure whether she was going to miss the house or me more, but I got caught up in the emotion of the moment and turned into a regular watering pot, crying right along with her.

After I was loaded in the truck, Grandpa got in behind the wheel. He rolled his window down and stuck his arm out. "Now Phoebe, Ola and I will be by in the morning to pick you up," he said to Mrs. Estes. "Don't you worry about a thing. We'll keep an eye out on your house for you."

This was my favorite time, just Grandpa and me. Grandma was all business. I guess because so many people counted on her, she couldn't show a soft side very often. But Grandpa was all kindness. He was more approachable and easier to talk to than Grandma. He must have known how difficult it was for me to let Mrs. Estes go, so he started talking about something else to take my mind off my sadness.

"Guess this will be a busy week," he mused.

"You mean Thanksgiving?" I asked. We would get out of school on Thursday, and every kid was looking forward to that, including me.

"Well there's that, but we might have something more going on," he answered.

I guess whatever was going to happen, I would be in the thick of it. After all, I wouldn't be staying with Mrs. Estes any more. "What else are we going to be doing?" I asked.

"It's a little early in the season, but the weather is just right to butcher the hogs -- no longer warm, but not freezing. You know what that means, don't you?"

Butchering hogs meant a whole lot, mainly a heap load of work, but I was guessing that work wasn't what Grandpa was talking about. "What's that Grandpa?"

"We'll be living high on the hog. That's what it means," he chuckled. Any butcher knew that the best, most tender meat is on the top, along the backbone. That part of the hog is called the tenderloin. As much as I liked pan fried tenderloin, what I couldn't wait for was a taste of the fresh, hot, crispy cracklings. We would indeed be living high on the hog.

If it was Grandpa's plan to take my mind off losing my job and Mrs. Estes, he succeeded. Suddenly, the week seemed very exciting. "That should make for a special Thanksgiving," I said.

Grandpa and I unloaded the sewing machine just as soon as we got home. Grandma was awake and Fenetta took up whining right where she left off before church started. "Momma, where in the world does she think we are going to put that thing?" she wailed.

Fenetta was barking up the wrong tree. Grandma had wanted a treadle sewing machine for longer than she could remember. "Don't worry about it crowding your bedroom," she responded. "We'll put it right here in the living room."

Even though there was work to be done, Grandma found some flour sacks to practice on and tried out my new sewing machine. All of us girls gathered round as she worked to get the hang of pumping the peddle, keeping the material straight, and most importantly – not running over her finger with the needle. It made me feel especially proud that I had already mastered this task. I wanted to dig through the patterns, find some material, and start making a dress. Momma gently suggested that I start out with something simple, like handkerchiefs. She promised to show me how to crochet a shell pattern around the edge to make them look pretty. By the time we went to bed, I had used a soft blue flour sack to make five ladies handkerchief. Momma showed me how to punch the crochet needle into the fabric and crochet the delicate lace around the edge. We were all surprised when Wanda showed an interest in the crocheting. She picked it up real quickly and made the neatest stitches of us all. Melba and I talked about embroidering a little flower in the corner of each handkerchief to make them extra special. We would have worked through the night, but Momma made us go to bed.

The next afternoon, I wanted to run all the way home so I could get started on my project. When we finally got there, we found that Grandpa and Daddy had butchered three hogs and there was a passel of work to be done for everyone.

"Jean, your grandpa is out in the smoke house. Go see if there is anything you can do to help him," Momma instructed. Before she could change her mind, I lit out to the smoke house and quickly stepped inside. I found Grandpa hanging the hams from the rafters. My feet slid on the dirt flour as I skidded to a stop inside the door.

"Well there you are, Sweetie," Grandpa said, like he had been looking for me. "I sure could use some help. Do you think you could find me a few good sized rocks?"

I was always eager to please Grandpa. "Sure, what do you need them for?" I asked.

"Grandpa pointed to a shallow pit he had dug in the middle of the dirt floor. "I'm going to build a fire in this pit so that these hams can get nice and smokey."

Yum, I loved smoked ham. "I'll be back in a flash," I said and headed out to search for just the right kind of rocks.

It ended up taking me a good hour to get enough rocks of the right size for that fire pit. When I carried in the last one, Grandpa placed the wood inside the circle and started the fire. He had several small chips of wood in a bucket and he liberally sprinkled those on the top of the flames.

"Grandpa, why did you chunk up that wood so small?" I asked.

He ushered me out of the smokehouse and closed the door tight. "Those chips are hickory wood. They give the meat a good, smoky kind of sweet flavor. The key will be to keep the door closed as much as possible. It's just like baking a cake. If you fan the oven door, it takes a lot longer for the cake to get done. Same here."

Grandpa picked up a bucket full of something that looked horrible bad and headed to the house. "What's in there?" I asked pointing to the bucket.

"That's chitlins," he answered. It was years before I learned that "chitlins" were actually pronounced "chitterlings." "We're taking these to Ms. Eunice. Your grandma is a saving woman, but she won't have chitlins in her house."

"Why?" I asked. "What's wrong with them?"

"Chittlins are the intestines," he answered.

"Intestines? Do you mean guts?" I was speechless. Surely not even Ms. Eunice was desperate enough to eat pig guts.

Grandpa got a smile on his face. "Don't get me wrong. There isn't a better neighbor than Ms. Eunice Williams, but that woman will cook plumb near anything. She's not the only one who likes chiltlins. Lots of people round about here like 'em."

"But Grandpa, aren't the guts full of . . . stuff?" I couldn't imagine anyone eating the undigested or partially digested food inside of an animal's intestines. Daddy had warned me about even rupturing the intestines while cleaning the animal. He said that what was in the intestines was dangerous for humans.

"Here's what Ms. Eunice will do," he explained. "She'll take these chitlins outside and she'll sling them around and around until she gets all of the stuff in there out. Next she'll wash them several times. When she is sure they are as clean as she can get them, she'll get two big iron pots out in her backyard."

This was still just unbelievable to me. "It doesn't look like we have too many. How come she'll need two pots, and why does she cook them outside?"

Grandpa chuckled. "I'll tell you why. Chitlins stink to high heaven. She'll boil them in one pot and then batter and fry them in the other, and she doesn't want that smell in her house."

As we rounded the house, we saw the women all gathered around a big pot out in our backyard. I drew nearer to see what was going on and got there just in time to see Grandma dip the first serving of crunchy cracklings out of the sizzling fat.

"Not yet," Aunt Lorene was warning Jerry as he reached for a bite. "You have to wait for them to cool off."

Most of the cooking oil for the year came from this once-a-year event. The fat from the hog was trimmed away from the meat and put into an iron pot over a medium fire. The heat caused the fat to break down and become liquid. When the fat was properly cooked, it became lard. That heating process, called rendering, preserved the fat and made it usable for the entire coming year. That lard was used to fry potatoes, chicken, make flaky pie crust, and anything else that required fat. It was near impossible to remove all of the skin from the pig before starting the lard rendering process. Tiny little pieces of those pigskins would sizzle in the hot oil and when fully cooked, they would float to the top of the pot. Everybody called them cracklings because they crackled when you bit into them. They were pure dee delicious.

"Jean," Grandpa called to me. "Do you want to go with me to take these chitlins over to Ms. Eunice?"

I was torn. Cracklins or going somewhere with Grandpa? Deciding that the treats had cooled enough, I grabbed a handful and took out after Grandpa. Thank goodness Grandpa put the chitlins in the back of the truck. The smell would have put me off from eating my cracklins. Although I wanted to save all of those delicious treats for myself, I offered to share with Grandpa. We had just finished them off as we pulled into the Williams's yard.

Grandpa hopped up onto the running board on the side of the truck and reached into the back for the chitlins. I jumped down from the truck and wiped my greasy hands on the grass. The dress I was wearing wasn't my new one, but I still didn't want to ruin it. Ms. Eunice was wiping her hands on her apron as she walked out on the porch to meet us. "Hello," she waved to us as we got closer. "What you got there?"

"Hey Ms. Eunice," Grandpa greeted her. "We brought you some chitlins."

"Why, it's not yet December. What are you doing butchering hogs so early?" she wanted to know.

"We decided to get an early start. Ola's almanac says the cold weather is going to start now and last through the whole winter," he answered.

Ms. Eunice hurried down the steps and took the bucket from Grandpa's hand. "Well, we know what I'll be doing this afternoon. Chitlins can't wait. Say, would y'all like to come over for dinner tonight. There's nothing better than fresh chitlins."

I learned something that day about the differences between men and women. Women might feel obliged to accept an invitation, no matter how bad they want to decline, but men just speak their minds.

"Now, Ms. Eunice," Grandpa said kindly. "You know we can't stand the smell of chitlins. That's the reason we bring them to you."

Ms. Eunice didn't seem offended. "Well at least let me boil you up some tasty hot tamales," she offered.

"Now, tamales sound mighty good, but we're the ones with the fresh pork. Let's fix them at our house. I'll have Ola get in touch with you. If you don't have family coming for Thanksgiving, we could do it then."

"We'll potluck," Ms. Eunice yelled as Grandpa and I headed to the truck.

And before she could argue, we were in the truck and heading back to the house.

"Boy, that was a close one," Grandpa laughed with relief. "Your Grandma would never have forgiven me if I had accepted an invitation to let Ms. Eunice feed us. Of course, now I've committed us to a hot tamale cook."

Talking about other folks and keeping harmless little secrets is part of the glue that keeps a family together. Even at eleven years old, I understood this. "After she almost poisoned poor little Clark, I would say that cooking for her is the lesser of two evils."

Grandpa cackled at that, which made me smile even more. I liked to make him happy.

Grandma seemed unfazed that Grandpa had extended an invitation. She even asked him if he would like to invite the McCloud's. Grandpa and Mr. McCloud were good friends, and I suspected that Grandma wanted another family to potluck with us, so it wouldn't be as noticeable when we didn't eat whatever food Ms. Eunice brought. Wanda was on cloud nine. This was another great opportunity for her to spend time with Willy.

That night, Momma put some cracklins into the cornbread. It added a crunchy delicious texture that made the taste buds sing. "Pass me some more of that cracklin bread," Grandpa said. This was his third piece. With a little melted butter on top, it was delicious.

Chapter Fourteen

An Exotic Dinner

Making hot tamales is an art, which takes a great deal of planning. The preparations started back a few months earlier when the corn was ready for harvest. The corncobs weren't the only thing of use on the stalk. When we prepared the corn for cooking and canning, Grandma showed us how to save the shucks that had surrounded the corn. We laid them out on the drying sheet, along with the fruit. Now that it was time to make hot tamales, we could put them to use.

Early on Thanksgiving morning, Grandma, Momma, and Aunt Lorene started boiling the meat. It was mostly pork, but there was some rabbit mixed in, too. The heavy rain had flooded the bottomland down by the river. Daddy had taken Grandpa's boat down there and hunted swamp rabbits. When the bottoms flooded, many of the rabbits were trapped. They found whatever clumps of driftwood they could and hopped aboard. This made hunting real easy. Daddy just had to paddle among the driftwood and pluck the rabbits right out. The tender white rabbit meat made the tamales extra tasty.

About mid morning, the meat was done and we older kids were able to get in on the whole process. Grandma had a hand grinder, which she attached to the edge of the kitchen table with the clamp and screw that were built onto the bottom of the grinder. We placed a rag between the table and clamp to protect the wood. The cooked meat was de-boned and then fed into the mouth of the grinder.

"Be careful to keep your fingers out of the grinder," Momma reminded us yet again.

"We will," all of us responded in tired voices. She had warned us so many times that we lost count.

Even though it was hard work, I loved getting to turn the handle and produce the ground meat needed for the tamales. When Aunt Lorene added some dried red peppers, the meat started to look more and more like the familiar tamale filling was supposed to.

"Can't we help?" Clark whined to his mommy.

"Sure," Aunt Lorene answered. "If you and Jerry will go get some onions, I'll let you take a turn at the grinder."

Normally, the boys would have complained about this unpleasant task, but the promise of being able to use the grinder was enough to send them off on their errand without one complaint.

Grandma and Grandpa didn't have an underground cellar, so their fall root vegetables like potatoes, turnips, and onions were stored under the front porch. Grandpa had dug down a little ways into the earth and lined the porch with two stacks of big rocks. Melba and I hated to go under there. Wanda just flat out refused that tasks, and as usual no one argued with her. It was dark under the porch, and I was always sure that snakes probably used the spot to den for the winter. At the very least, there were most certainly spiders. As quick as a flash, Clark and Jerry came back with three nice looking onions and one that was starting to rot.

Momma pealed them all, being careful to get all of the mushy part off the one that was going bad. The boys couldn't wait to get their chance at the grinder. The job looked easy when an adult was turning the crank, but little boys with small muscles found the work much harder than expected. Clark did about five turns all by himself before he gave out. Aunt Lorene helped Jerry turn the crank and then gradually stopped helping until he was struggling to get the crank around even one time. After they found out that it was more work than fun, they lost interest and went into the living room to play. Since the weather had turn off cold, we were all stuck in the crowded house. Every time I turned around, it seemed like I was getting in someone's way.

A big pan sat underneath the grinder to catch the meat as it came out. Grandma made sure that all of the ingredients were mixed real well before adding salt and some of the broth from the meat. A pot of cornmeal mush simmered on the stove. The mush was made from meat broth and a little bit of cornmeal. The dried corn shucks were set to soak in a bucket of warm water, making them pliable when the time came to use them.

The Williams's and McCloud's arrived around eleven o'clock, just in time to help put the hot tamales together. We set up two assembly lines and went to work. On our line, Melba spread out a thin layer of mush over one of the corn shucks. She scooted it over to me where I placed a narrow line of the ground meat on the inside and handed it to Wanda. She folded the shuck over and wrapped another one around it. Grandma inspected each one and then tied off the ends with a small piece of twine, which she had saved from the flour sacks. Once all of the tamales were ready, they went into a pot of boiling water. Within a few minutes, they were ready to dip out of the pot and cool.

Momma went out to draw more water from the well and made us girls go with her. "But I want to help," I complained. "You won't need all of us to get water."

She squinted up her eyes and used her stern voice. "You will do as I say right now," she said. Momma didn't talk like this very often, so I knew that she meant business.

Just as soon as we got out of the house, Momma dropped her voice. "Ms. Eunice made the cobbler and the corn bread. Don't eat either one of them."

None of us had to be told twice. Visions of Clark's rice pudding danced in our memories.

"What about Mrs. McCloud?" Melba whispered.

Wanda put her hands on her hips and tapped her foot. "There's nothing wrong with the food she brought," she said between gritted teeth. I guess no one was allowed to question her boyfriend's family.

Momma gently patted her shoulder. "According to your grandma, she's as clean as can be. She brought the pinto beans and light bread."

I couldn't help but do a little hop of joy. Light bread was a store bought loaf of bread that was already precut. We didn't get many opportunities to eat that light-as-air treat. I sure would have hated to find out that for some reason or another we weren't able to partake of it.

The hardest part about fixing hot tamales is waiting until they cool enough to eat. If they are opened up too soon, the tamale doesn't hold together. But if they are allowed to cool down for thirty minutes or more, the tamale rolls right out of the cornhusk shell.

Since there wasn't anything left to do in the kitchen, everybody gathered in the living room with the men. Mr. McCloud was talking, and we sat quietly to listen.

"I planned on bringing my bagpipe with me tonight," he said. "Thought we might have some music after dinner. When I went to get it, the mice had chewed holes all in it. My great granddaddy brought it over from Scotland. I sure am going to miss its sweet sound."

I noticed Aunt Lorene elbow Momma and then both of them got tickled. Mrs. McCloud glared at them and shook her head.

"I think I'll check on the tamales," Aunt Lorene said by way of excusing herself.

Momma followed her. Being a little bit nosey, I snuck in behind them and stood quietly by the door. Both women were doubled up with laughter.

My curiosity got the best of me, and I couldn't help but try to find out why they were tickled. "What's so funny?" I asked.

Mommy looked up and put her finger to her lips to silence me. She motioned me over and answered in a low voice. "Mr. McCloud can't play the bagpipe worth nothing, so Mrs. McCloud took the scissors to it and told him that a mouse had gotten into it."

"We sure are mighty grateful," Aunt Lorene added. "Tamales go down a lot better if you don't have to put up with his caterwauling."

"Don't get me wrong," Momma suddenly remembered that they were talking to a kid. "Mr. McCloud's as good as gold, but his playing is enough to raise the dead."

Aunt Lorene nodded in agreement. "Do you remember the last year I was at home Jean? Everybody went home from the Forth of July picnic with a pounding headache?"

"Yup. What Mrs. McCloud did was a relief to the whole community. We wouldn't want to get her in trouble by blabbering about it."

The dining table was a long plank table. A bench ran along the whole length of the side closest to the wall. Two big chairs were placed at each end and five smaller chairs were lined up on the other side. Grandpa sat at one end, with the men close to him while Grandma sat at the other end with the women close to her. The kids scooted across the bench until it was plumb crowded. There was hardly any wiggle room between us. Wanda and her boyfriend, Willy McCloud, did their best to make it easier on us. They sat real close together. Once I looked under the table and saw that they were holding hands. Fenetta must have resented the fact that Wanda's boyfriend was allowed to visit and hers wasn't, because she glared daggers at Wanda all night long. I was real glad for Wanda. She seemed happier than I had ever seen her.

Thanksgiving dinner was a tasty change from our regular meals. We loved fruits and vegetables from the garden, and we frequently had meat, but the tamales were a little more exotic tasting than our regular meals. By the time we left the table, every tamale had been devoured.

Ms. Eunice got up to help the women clear the table. "There are still a bunch of cornbread and cobbler left. Does anyone want another helping?"

Grandpa patted his stomach. "Couldn't eat another bite," he announced. Everyone else agreed.

"Well, I guess I'll just have to warm it over tomorrow for dinner. Maybe I'll kill a bird and fix some chicken and dressing with it. I'm pretty sure my old rooster isn't long for this world. He's been acting funny lately, so I might as well use him before he dies on me," she said as she put away most of the cornbread she had brought.

It didn't take long to get the dishes cleaned. As we re-joined the men in the living room, Mr. McCloud was still lamenting the fact that he couldn't play his bagpipe.

"If you're really set on some music, I could drag out my fiddle," Grandpa offered. That perked Mr. McCloud right up. As Grandpa sawed out a tune, Mr. McCloud showed us how to dance a Scottish dance. It was a lot of skipping and hopping, and we caught onto the steps right away.

Daddy and Mr. Williams disappeared outside for a long time. When they came back in, there was a strong odor of alcohol on Daddy's breath. Melba and I moved to the other side of the room and sat real close to each other. Grandpa took a break and sat down beside us.

"What's the matter pumpkin?" he asked Melba.

She looked down and away. "Daddy smells funny," she whispered.

I was angry that he was doing this again. Things had been so good since we had been here with Grandma and Grandpa. "He's been drinking," I added. "You know what that means."

Grandpa didn't say anything more. Before long, our little Thanksgiving party broke up. We got ready for bed and quietly settled in for the night. Before I fell asleep, I heard Grandpa and Daddy talking outside. I couldn't make out the words, but I could tell that Grandpa was upset. After a few minutes, Grandpa came back inside, but Daddy never did. I don't know where he slept that night or what he did, but he was back in the morning. No one acted like anything was wrong and everything went back to normal. It was only a short time before we were getting ready for another upset.

Chapter Fifteen

Going Home

Something big was going on. Melba and I caught Momma and Daddy whispering several times, but every time they caught sight of us, they hushed up real fast. With Thanksgiving behind us and Christmas right around the corner, Wanda, Melba and I were working hard on our Christmas gifts. The treadle sewing machine had opened up a whole new world for us. In the patterns, we found an apron pattern. Even though I wouldn't tell her why I needed them, Grandma dug into her storehouse of feed and flour sacks and let me use whatever I needed. I especially liked the sacks that flour came in, because they were softer and sometimes had pretty printed designs.

I sewed aprons for the women and handkerchiefs for the men, and Melba embroidered on them. She picked flowers and bird patterns for the ladies and simple initial patterns for the men. Grandpa got a black "J" on his for

Jon, and Daddy got a "B" for Bill. We even made smaller handkerchiefs for Clark and Jerry. Wanda crocheted beautiful lace for the bottom of the aprons. Since that was an extra hard job, Melba and I agreed to put Wanda's name on the gifts for the men, even though she didn't work on those. In keeping with the holiday spirit, Melba and I made two handkerchiefs for Willie McCloud as a present from Wanda. Being around that boy seemed to make her happier and more eager to get along. Sometimes days stretched without a fight between her and Fenetta.

On December 11, 1936, the world was rocked with the news that the King of England, Edward the VIII, had abdicated his throne. We all sat around the radio and listened as the serious report was read. None of us could believe that he would give up being king just so he could marry a woman. Personally, I thought that his wife, Wallis Simpson would have made a good queen. I don't know why I thought this; it just seemed the loyal thing to believe. After all, the woman was an American. The reason she was considered unacceptable probably had more to do with the fact that she was divorced than it did that she wasn't a British citizen. It seemed to me that maybe this news perked Aunt Lorene up a little bit. After all, if a divorcee could snag the king of England, there might be a chance for her to find a good man. The divorce papers had arrived from Uncle Jim back a month or so ago. Even though she cried and cried when she read them, Aunt Lorene didn't waste any time signing them and sending them back. Momma said that it would take a year or more for it to be official.

Christmas was just around the corner, and everyone was getting excited. Mrs. Russell brought a Sears Roebuck catalog to school and showed us how to make snowflakes out of the paper.

"Fold two pieces of paper together," Mrs. Russell said as she demonstrated with two pages of her own. "Fold it again and again and again."

"Like this?" Ina Lee Jackson asked from the front row.

Mrs. Russell walked over to inspect Ina Lee's work. "Fold it one more time," she instructed. The room erupted with questions.

"What about mine, Mrs. Russell? Does this look okay?"

"Mrs. Russell, come look at this one."

"I tore one of my pages. Can I have another one?"

One by one, our patient teacher answered every question. Sometimes I wondered if she had nerve problems like Grandma. With all of us kids vying for her attention, there was a good chance. Finally, everyone's paper was folded just right.

"Okay, when you get the scissors, cut it like this." Once again, Mrs. Russell demonstrated. The questions started all over again.

"Can I use the scissors first?"

"I'm not a very good cutter. Will you help me?"

"Start the scissors on this side of the room. That side always gets to go first."

The true Christmas miracle of the year was that every kid finally finished the snowflakes, and we had a present to take home for our families. Once the family aprons and handkerchiefs were finished, we worked on gifts for our teachers. We must have been feeling especially good spirited, because we even let Fenetta talk us into making a handkerchief for her teacher. It was one that Melba had messed up a little on the embroidering, giving the bird three legs. If she ripped out the thread, little holes would have remained in the fabric. Fenetta didn't seem to notice, and we didn't mention it. On Christmas Eve, Melba, Wanda, and I decided that we had been mean spirited not to make a gift for Fenetta. In a rare moment of kindness, Wanda drug out a big peppermint stick Willy had given her and wrapped it up for her annoying aunt.

"I bet she won't have anything for us," Wanda predicted. She was right, but we didn't let it bother us.

Christmas morning dawned bright and clear. Even though we had dreamed about a white Christmas, the weather was actually kind of warm for the season. Grandma put on a ham for dinner and Melba and I were sent to get some sweet potatoes and onions out from under the porch. There was no meat grinder to entice the boys into doing the job this time. A board covered the opening on the end. We moved it aside and got the vegetables out as quickly as we could.

After dinner, we settled in to open our presents. Every one of us kids got a new coat. Because the girls were all pretty close to the same size, Momma had sewn our names into the tags. She was pretty smart about finding ways to head off arguments before they started. Melba got some pretty embroidery threads. Pretty pink crochet thread was wrapped up for Wanda, and I got a new Butterick dress pattern in my size. In addition to her new coat, Fenetta got a new bible. If Melba had offered, I think Fenetta would have traded her special gift for some embroidery threat. As excited as we were about the gifts we received, I was even more eager to see what everyone thought of the presents we had made for them.

"Oh girls," Grandma gushed. "This is the most beautiful apron I've ever seen. I'll be afraid to use it in the kitchen. It's just too pretty. I'll have to save it for special occasions."

"I embroidered the bird," Melba piped up.

Even Wanda wanted to get in on the praise. "Jean sewed them, and I did the lace, just like you showed me, Momma."

Momma carefully examined her apron. "You girls did a wonderful job. It must have taken you hours. Thank you!" She hugged each one of us and let us know that she loved us.

Aunt Lorene followed right behind her. "This makes me wish I had little girls," she whispered in my ear as she squeezed me tight. I knew she loved the boys and wouldn't trade them for love or money, but she made us feel special anyway.

Daddy folded his handkerchief and quietly tucked it into his pocket. Grandpa traced the letter "J" with his finger. "Fancy thing like this, my friends might think I've gotten uppity. They might think we're right up there with the Rockefellers."

The Rockefellers were rich, maybe even super rich. We knew that Grandpa was just teasing. We teased back just to let him know how much we loved him.

"Well, if you're afraid to use it," Wanda said. "Maybe we should just give it to Mr. McCloud. I bet he would appreciate it."

Grandpa let on that he thought Wanda was being serious. "No way am I going to let Mr. McCloud get his hands on this pretty thing. If anybody gets to mess up this fancy nose rag, it's going to be me."

Clark got a truck made out of tin, and Jerry got a tractor. They couldn't have cared less about the handkerchiefs we had made them, but it didn't hurt our feelings. They were just little boys.

"There's one last present," Daddy said when all the gifts had been opened. "I've got a job. We're moving back home."

It was so quiet that we could have heard a pin drop. No one said a word. Wanda was the one who finally broke the silence.

"I'm not going," she said. Her arms were folded over her chest and she had that stubborn look that spelled trouble. "I'm staying with Grandma and Grandpa."

"Me too. I'm staying too." I screamed in my heart. But not a word came out as I sat silent and numb.

Daddy got up and towered over Wanda. Because we were still living in Grandpa's house, he didn't threaten her. He just talked real firmly. "We're moving," he said. "All of us." With that he pushed out the front door and let the screen door slam behind him.

"I'm not going," Wanda repeated to no one in particular. "We are happy here, and I'm not moving."

Momma didn't say a word. She just sat there with her head bowed down. I could tell that she was thinking the same thing I was. The drinking would start again and so would the beatings. Every time he was late getting home from work, we would be going to bed early. One thing was for sure, the gifts were forgotten. The season of giving was over. Christmas was ruined.

It took five days, but Daddy was as good as his word. We packed up and moved back across the Black River, all of us - even Wanda. When Daddy finally laid down the law to her, she whispered something to him that made his face turn white. Later, I asked her what she had said.

"I told him that everybody has to sleep sometime, and if he ever whipped me again, he might not wake up some morning."

I spent most of my life being a little bit afraid of Wanda, but at times like this I wished I had just a little of her courage. She never again went to bed early, and Daddy never took his belt to her.

When the time came, Grandpa's pickup truck was packed up again. This time it was more crowded. Our possessions had grown while we lived with Grandma and Grandpa. My treadle sewing machine was the biggest addition. I saw Grandma eyeing it as it was loaded and felt guilty about taking it with me, but not so guilty that I even once considered leaving it.

Grandpa sat quietly behind the wheel, waiting for us to load into the truck. The rest of us were hugging and crying and saying our goodbyes. Even Fenetta gave us all a rare hug and told us that she would miss us. Of course, we all knew that was a lie, but it was nice of her just the same. Finally, it was time to go. Momma sat next to Grandpa with Melba and me on her lap. Wanda sat on Daddy's lap and he didn't once complain about her bony butt cutting into his legs, even though I knew from experience that she was causing him some substantial pain.

The fear of what awaited us overshadowed the fear of getting across the river by ferry. There was no smiling Bill Dentrick to wave us on or off. Grandpa didn't offer to take me out to watch the fish and turtles, but as we sat packed together in that truck, he took my hand and gave it a gentle squeeze. That sweet show of love and affection both comforted me and set me over the edge. My throat tightened up until it hurt and my lip trembled as I did my best to control my urge to break down and cry.

We didn't go back to the house by the Millers. It had already been rented out to some other family. The new house was even bigger and nicer than Grandma and Grandpa's. It was two stories, but Daddy warned us that the upstairs wasn't completed. The stairs hadn't even been built.

We all helped unload the truck. Daddy and Grandpa lifted the heavy stuff, while we took care of the boxes. They didn't talk much to each other, just went about getting the job done.

"How can we afford this?" I heard Momma ask Daddy.

Daddy nodded to the front hall where brown spots stained the wall and floor. "The owner was killed here. We'll have to clean up the blood where it happened, but it's a good house."

Momma nervously put her hand to her throat. "Killed?" she said. "How?"

Daddy shrugged. "All I know is that people see lights in the house at night. They think it's haunted, so nobody else would buy or rent it. We're getting it for a song."

"But Bill," Momma argued.

"Ruby, it's the best we can do," he answered. That was it. End of argument.

Before we knew it, everything was unloaded, and Grandpa was ready to go. Momma hugged him long and hard before he got in the truck. "Thank you for taking us in Papa," she said.

He looked into her eyes for a long time. It was like he was trying to send her a silent message. "Ruby, you know we're always here for you. You're always welcome."

Wanda and Melba were next in line to get their hugs, and finally it was time for me. I grabbed hold of Grandpa and didn't want to let him go. When I finally slacked up my grip, he didn't say anything. "Grandpa," I started to speak but I couldn't get anything else out.

"I know, Sugar, I know," he choked out, and for the second time, I saw him cry. His voice quivered, but he kept on talking. "But no matter whether it's a grand adventure or the worst day of your life, you are not by yourself. You are *never* by yourself. The good Lord's with you and as long as I have breath in my body, so am I."

Momma went on into the house and got busy cleaning up the dried blood. But Wanda, Melba, and I stood and waved goodbye to Grandpa until his truck rounded a bend and drove out of sight.

That night, we learned what made the strange lights in the house. Jackson County farmland was flat, except for the levy that protected the town if the river flooded out of its banks. When a car drove up and over that manmade rise, the headlights shined through the windows making it look from the outside like lights dancing inside the house. Ghosts were not what kept us awake and shaking with fear at night. It was something real.

We were excited to learn that the house had three bedrooms. Momma told Wanda that as the oldest, she could have her own bedroom. Melba and I were surprised when she turned it down to share a room with us.

"Someone has to protect you two," she said by way of explanation. She might boss us around and treat us like her personal servants, but she tried to the best of her ability to do what she could to look out for us. We turned the third bedroom into our sewing room.

Come the next election, Arkansas got a new governor. The Highway Department went back to work and Daddy slipped back into his old ways. For many years, there was no protecting Momma. When things were at their worst, I dreamed about that happy time with Grandma and Grandpa and wished we were back there.

My letters to Mrs. Estes often became my lifeline. Sometimes it's only possible to pour out your hopes, dreams and fears on paper. Instead of a diary, which I was sure Wanda would find and read, I wrote to my former employer and benefactor about the horrible things that happened in our house.

Her words of wisdom still fill my mind when I think about the ups and downs life has to offer.

"*Dear Jean,*" she wrote. "*Sometimes life is like those head lice you told me about back last summer. It's pure ole misery and you get so tired, you could just break down and give up. But other times, it's like those spicy, mouth-watering hot tamales you had for Thanksgiving, something rare and exciting. Just remember that as long as you love and are loved back, it's all worth it. Maybe looking forward to the hot tamales gets you through the head lice."*

More than once, we were sure that momma wouldn't make it through one of those terrible beatings. Like all families, the years brought us our fair share of heartbreak, but we had joys that made it all worth living.

We realized shortly after leaving Newark that daddy should have waited to share his name with a son. One after another, momma gave us three wonderful brothers.

The things we learned and the relationships we forged during that summer with grandma and grandpa served us well through life.

Melba went on to become the healthcare professional that grandma Marshall inspired her to be, heading up the surgical nursing unit at the veterans' hospital in Poplar Bluff, Missouri.

While Wanda was truly one of the smartest women I have ever known, life was never easy for her. She had two lovely children and a marriage that had more downs than ups. No matter how hard things became, Wanda crocheted gifts for family and friends until shortly before her death.

Life became almost unbearable for our family by the time I was sixteen. Seeing no way out, I ran off with a widower who was eleven years older than me. For the next several years, my heart and house were always full

155

as I raised nine children who have filled my life with love. Life has often been a roller coaster, with more than its share of head lice moments, but oh how wonderful are the hot tamale events.

When I look in the mirror at my wrinkles and white hair, I wonder where all the time went. When I close my eyes, I can still feel grandpa's warm hug and inhale the scent of grape juice, rose petals and honest sweat.

The End

52209375R00088

Made in the USA
Lexington, KY
22 May 2016